ADAM AND EVE IN THE GARDEN:
A 21ST CENTURY LOVE STORY
JUST THE TWO OF US

CHUKKY DANIELS

Published by: AR PRESS
Roger L. Brooks, Publisher
roger@americanrealpublishing.com
americanrealpublishing.com

Table of Contents

This historical fiction is intended to allow for a deep exploration of the Adam and Eve narrative with a modern twist, touching on autonomy, ethics, partnership, feminist interpretations, love and romance, and environmental lessons that are embedded in the Adam and Eve story.

The purpose of this book is to educate, to challenge, and to entertain. The author and the publisher do not warrant that the information contained in this book is fully complete and shall not be held responsible for any errors or omissions. The author and publisher shall have neither liability nor responsibility to any person or entity with respect to any loss or emotional discomfort caused or alleged to be caused directly or indirectly by reading this book.

This book ends with the birth of Adam and Eve's first child, setting the stage for a sequel that would delve deeper into their life outside Eden, the intricate dynamics of their family, and the legacy of their decisions.

INTRODUCTION:
The Garden's Whisper

In Eden's glow where rivers flow,
Where golden fruit and flowers grow,
Two lovers walked with no concern,
No sorrow known that I'll confirm.

The Tree of Life in splendour grew,
Branches bathed in the morning's hue.
Yet near it stood, in all its might,
The Tree of Knowledge in clear sight.

The serpent stirred with cunning gaze,
And whispered low in twisted praise,
"Why fear the fruit that calls your name?
Why shun the gift that sparks the flame?"

With trembling hands, with breath held tight,
Eve reached into the dappled light.
The forbidden fruit—so smooth, so red,
Upon her lips its sweetness spread.

Then Adam stood, his heart unsure,
Yet drawn by love so deep, so pure.
He took, he ate, and in one breath,
They met their fate, they tasted death.

The Fall had come, their eyes made wide,
No place to run, no veil to hide.
The Garden wept, the heavens sighed,
As love now bore the weight of pride.

Yet through the dust, through toil and pain,
Humanity would rise again.
For love endured, though lost was peace,
And through the dark, sought new release.

In the beginning, the world was a paradise, untouched by the stain of imperfection. In its heart lay a garden—Eden—a sanctuary of eternal beauty, where every leaf, every petal, every breeze carried the whispers of creation's perfection. It was here, amidst the tranquil symphony of life, that the story of humanity's origins unfolded.

But paradise is never truly without its shadows. In Eden, there were two extraordinary trees: one offering eternal life and the other, the forbidden knowledge of good and evil. Adam and Eve, the first humans, lived in innocent harmony, blissfully unaware of the choices that lay ahead. Yet, temptation is as ancient as time itself, and the serpent's cunning whispers would ignite a cascade of events that would forever alter the fabric of humanity's existence.

For the first time in history, someone is bold enough to dive deeper and discuss the controversial, romantic, and sensitive aspects of the Adam and Eve story. In this bold and provocative reimagining of one of humanity's most ancient tales, Chukky Daniels takes readers back to the Garden of Eden to explore the timeless themes of love, choice, temptation, and consequence.

What sets this retelling apart is its exploration of the emotional and relational journey of Adam and Eve as they transition from siblings to lovers, grappling with guilt, passion, and the dawning realisation of their mortality. Together, they forge a family, laying the foundation for all who follow, yet bearing the weight of their choices.

This book ends with the birth of their first child, Cain, setting the stage for a sequel that will delve deeper into the dynamics of the Adam and Eve family and the legacy of their decisions.

WHY ARE PEOPLE STILL FASCINATED WITH THE STORY?

The story of Adam and Eve endures because it captures the universal essence of human experience. At its core, it is a narrative about choice, consequence, and the complexities of being human. This tale transcends religious or historical contexts to speak to our deepest curiosities and struggles.

In every generation, people wrestle with the same questions posed in Eden: What does it mean to seek knowledge? How do we reconcile the pursuit of autonomy with the responsibilities it brings? The story resonates because it mirrors our lives—the joys and sorrows of self-awareness, the challenges of moral accountability, and the enduring quest for meaning in a world shaped by our decisions.

PURPOSE AND MODERN RELEVANCE OF THE STORY

This retelling of Adam and Eve's journey is not merely a recounting of an ancient tale—it is an exploration of themes that remain profoundly relevant in our contemporary world. Curiosity, autonomy, and the pursuit of consciousness are as central to human existence today as they were in Eden. In an era in which information abounds and choices are endless, the story serves as a mirror, reflecting humanity's enduring struggle to balance knowledge, freedom, and moral responsibility.

By delving into the lives of the first humans, we are reminded of the timeless questions that shape our existence: What drives us to seek understanding? How do we navigate the consequences of our choices? And what does it mean to reconcile love with loss, guilt with forgiveness?

OVERVIEW OF THEMES: CURIOSITY, AUTONOMY, AND CONSCIOUSNESS

Curiosity: The serpent's allure, the forbidden fruit, and the fateful decision to eat from the Tree of Knowledge highlight humanity's innate drive to question, explore, and understand. This theme resonates in today's world, where the pursuit of knowledge can bring both enlightenment and unforeseen consequences.

Autonomy: Adam and Eve's journey is a testament to the power of choice. Their story underscores the complexities of free will—the courage it takes to act, the consequences of those actions, and the growth that emerges from navigating life's uncertainties.

Consciousness: With the first bite of the fruit, Adam and Eve awaken to the realities of good and evil, life and death, joy and sorrow. This awakening mirrors humanity's ongoing quest for self-awareness and the challenges of living in a world that demands both accountability and compassion.

WHAT MAKES THIS BOOK DIFFERENT:

Unique Perspective: A fresh retelling that humanises Adam and Eve, delving into their emotions, relationships, sexuality, and choices.

Broad Appeal: Themes of love, choice, and redemption resonate across religious, literary, and romantic fiction audiences.

Compelling Series Potential: With a sequel planned to explore the birth of Abel, the fratricide, and the birth of Seth, this story is poised to capture readers' imaginations over multiple books.

Through vivid storytelling and profound introspection, this book dares to challenge conventional narratives of Adam and Eve while exploring eternal themes. This timeless tale reimagined offers a lens through which to view humanity's origins on a journey into the heart of what it means to choose, to love, and to live.

Step into Eden. Witness the beginning and let the story whisper its truths to your soul.

CHAPTER 1:

The Creation and the Garden

The Garden of Eden story has deeply impacted art and culture, serving as inspiration for different artistic, literary, and philosophical works. From Renaissance masterpieces to modern-day renditions, the Eden story still captivates.

The Adam and Eve narrative in Genesis, an original myth of cosmic significance, describes the Creator's six-day formation of the world, leading up to—and including—the creation of the first humans, Adam and Eve. The ancient story explores themes such as creation, human purpose, and a divine relationship.

The biblical version of creation from Genesis 1 explains how God, in an organised and meaningful way, created the heavens, the earth, and life in six days. Over successive days, God brought various things into being and saw that each was good, according to His judgment. Here's a recap of what was created on each day:

DAY 1: LIGHT AND DARKNESS

On day one, God created light and called it "day," and the darkness He called "night." By separating light from darkness, time was instituted, and thus a first day came into being: one cycle of evening and morning. God's light pierced through the void, dramatically paving the way for all creation to follow.

DAY 2: THE SKY

On the second day, God created the sky to separate the waters above from the waters below. With this powerful act, the earthbound waters and wide sky were distinctly separated. God also began to provide a place for stars, planets, and eventually life itself. The sky was created as a necessary component of God's design so that it becomes a foundation on which the universe can evolve in all its majesty.

DAY 3: LAND, SEAS, AND VEGETATION

On the third day, God separated the waters to reveal dry land and commanded the land to produce vegetation, including plants and trees that bear seeds and fruit for reproduction. This marked the beginning of life on Earth, with plants and trees designed to multiply and provide sustenance for all living beings.

DAY 4: SUN, MOON, AND STARS

On the fourth day, God created the sun, the moon, and stars to provide light, regulate celestial motions, and establish patterns in nature, such as time progression and seasonal cycles.

DAY 5: FISH AND BIRDS

God created many sea creatures and birds on the fifth day. He blessed them with fertility, bringing into existence life as we know it. The waters and skies were filled with myriad lively creatures, marking a significant chapter in the creation narrative and bringing animation to that which God had made.

DAY 6: LAND ANIMALS AND HUMANITY

On the sixth day, God made all sorts of animals to live on land: livestock and things that crawl around. In a dramatic turn of events, God also formed Adam from dust and breathed life into him. This intimate creation sets man apart from all other creatures: it was this divine breath in Adam that gave him his spark. And God said, "Let us make man in our image and after our likeness…" (Genesis 1:26). Meaning: Let humanity evolve into godlike resemblance! Therefore, Genesis attests as a factual pillar to the reality that man is an expression of creative dominion.

THE GARDEN OF EDEN

After creating Adam, God made a Garden in Eden from the wide expanse of the Garden of the Universe, a veritable paradise teeming with life and pristine beauty. The Garden of Eden became a sacred space that encapsulated an idyllic state of being: Here, God and man dwelled together. Rivers ran through it, watering the garden so that life on the land was brought forth.

This Garden was animated by sounds of nature itself and God's presence, not just scenery. It was the perfect existence—an unspoiled world where humans communed directly with God. The Creator placed Adam in the Garden, and he was to tend it—all of creation, as defined by his stewardship over humanity.

THE SIGNIFICANCE OF THE GARDEN

The Garden of Eden symbolised the original state of humanity—innocent, free, and in harmony with the divine order. It reflected paradise, a place untouched by conflict or pain. Here, Adam enjoyed a relationship with God characterised by direct interaction and companionship. There were no barriers between the Creator and His creation; Adam walked with God in the cool of the day, experiencing the fullness of life in a world unmarred by fear or shame.

The garden also represented the balance between nature and humanity. Adam was not merely a passive inhabitant but an active caretaker, responsible for nurturing the land. This stewardship underscores the theme of interconnectedness—the idea that humanity is part of a larger ecosystem, tasked with preserving and respecting the world around it.

HUMANITY'S INTENDED RELATIONSHIP WITH NATURE

In the narrative, God commands Adam to "Be fruitful and multiply and fill the earth and subdue it," establishing a blueprint for humanity's interaction with creation. This directive conveys the importance of growth, responsibility, and care for the earth. The harmony of Eden serves as a model for what a respectful and nurturing relationship with nature should look like.

However, embedded in this idyllic scene is a foreshadowing of the complexities that will arise as humanity exercises its free will. The introduction of the Tree of Knowledge of Good and Evil—alongside the Tree of Life—will later become a critical point of conflict, highlighting the tension between divine commandments and human choice.

THE IDEAL STATE OF EXISTENCE

As we reflect on the creation narrative and the Garden of Eden, we encounter fundamental themes that resonate deeply within the human experience. The garden represents not only a physical paradise but also a spiritual state of being—an ideal where innocence, harmony, and divine presence coalesce.

In chapter 2, the foundation for understanding the significance of Eden in the broader context of the Adam and Eve story will be explored. The stage is set for the unfolding drama of choice, temptation, and the profound consequences of human actions. The allure of Eden beckons, inviting us to explore the depths of its narrative and the timeless lessons it imparts.

The story of Adam and Eve in the Garden of Eden is one of humanity's most captivating narratives, echoing through religious texts, literature, and art for millennia. It serves as a foundational myth, rich in themes of creation, choice, and the duality of human nature.

The allure of Eden lies not only in its idyllic representation of paradise but also in the profound lessons it offers regarding innocence, knowledge, temptation, and the quest for redemption. As we embark on this exploration, we will unravel the layers of this ancient story, revealing its significance in the spiritual and moral fabric of human existence.

The Garden of Eden is more than an ancient narrative; it is a profound exploration of the human soul, a tale that has captivated imaginations across millennia, touching on universal themes that resonate in the depths of human experience. The story of Eden, with Adam and Eve at its heart, is one of beauty and complexity, innocence and choice. Its telling—an account of paradise, a forbidden fruit, and the consequences that follow—invites readers into a realm where humanity's most fundamental questions of life, purpose, and identity come to life.

As depicted in the book of Genesis, Eden is an idyllic garden, a place of perfect harmony, where Adam and Eve dwell in innocence and in close communion with their Creator. Genesis presents Eden not merely as a physical paradise but as a symbol of humanity's original connection with the divine and with the natural world. For Adam and Eve, Eden is a place without pain or fear, where they live in pure harmony with themselves, each other, and their surroundings. Within its boundaries, they experience life in its fullest form, untouched by the complexity and hardship that would come later.

But this paradise is also a setting for an unfolding drama that will shape the human experience forever. When Adam and Eve encounter the Tree of Knowledge of Good and Evil, the tension between innocence and knowledge, obedience and freedom, surfaces. God has set a single boundary for Adam and Eve: not to eat from this tree. The arrival of the serpent, a figure embodying temptation, and the fateful choice made by Eve and later, Adam, represent moments of profound significance in the narrative. Their choice to eat the forbidden fruit transforms not only their own lives but also the trajectory of humanity.

What follows is their expulsion from Eden—a powerful symbol of the transition from innocence to awareness, from pure connection to a more complex, divided existence. In many ways, the Eden story is about the human journey, the discovery of our own capabilities, the burden of knowledge, and the quest to find our way back to meaning and connection, even after experiencing separation and exile.

THE ENDURING APPEAL OF EDEN'S STORY

In culture, there are some misconceptions about Adam and Eve as described in the book of Genesis. The infamous fruit they ate is not explicitly referred to as an apple. The serpent who entices Eve is not portrayed as the devil. Rather, it's described as a cunning creature. Initially, God forms Adam, followed by the creation of Eve later. They dwell in the Garden of Eden until succumbing to temptation and eating the fruit. As a result of their transgression being revealed by God, they are banished from the paradise garden and into the vast expanse of the Garden of the Universe.

Why has the story of Eden endured for so many centuries, captivating people across cultures and traditions? Part of its appeal lies in its universal themes: the innocence of paradise, the allure of forbidden knowledge, the weight of moral choices, and the consequences of those choices. These elements speak to the deepest parts of the human experience—our yearning for connection, our struggle with temptation, and our search for redemption and belonging.

Across religions, Eden has become a symbol of humanity's spiritual journey, often interpreted as an exploration of the relationship between humanity and the divine. In Christianity, it lays the foundation for concepts of sin and redemption, underscoring the belief in humanity's need for salvation and reconciliation with God.

In Judaism, the story emphasises the significance of moral choices and repentance, guiding adherents toward a life of responsibility and growth. In Islam, the Eden narrative reinforces themes of divine mercy, forgiveness, and human accountability. Even outside these religious contexts, Eden has inspired philosophical interpretations about human nature, freedom, and the meaning of knowledge and growth.

The story's symbolism also transcends religious boundaries. In literature, art, and music, the Garden of Eden has inspired countless interpretations that explore what it means to be human. It has become a canvas for reflecting on the human psyche, the nature of innocence, and the inevitability of change. From the poetry of John Milton's *Paradise Lost* to the rich artistic depictions of Adam and Eve in Renaissance art, the Eden story continues to inspire new ways of seeing and understanding ourselves.

THE CORE THEMES OF INNOCENCE, CHOICE, AND REDEMPTION

At the heart of the Eden narrative are several powerful themes that shape the human experience.

> **Innocence and Knowledge**: In Eden, Adam and Eve represent a state of purity, untouched by shame or guilt. This innocence symbolizes humanity's original, undivided state, where knowledge has not yet separated them from their Creator or from each other. The decision to eat from the Tree of Knowledge changes this innocence forever, and in doing so, illustrates the irreversible journey toward self-awareness, responsibility, and moral complexity.

> **Temptation and Moral Choice**: The serpent's presence in Eden embodies the force of temptation—a moment that reveals the power of curiosity and the allure of the unknown. Adam and Eve's choice to eat the forbidden fruit is a pivotal moment in the narrative, highlighting the complexity of human freedom. This choice reflects humanity's capacity for agency and self-determination, underscoring that choices come with both consequences and the potential for growth.

Exile and Struggle: The expulsion from Eden signifies humanity's transition from an ideal, harmonious existence to a world filled with hardship and struggle. This exile is both literal and symbolic: it represents not only the physical separation from paradise but also the spiritual and emotional journey that humanity must undergo. Outside Eden, Adam and Eve face pain, toil, and the realities of a life that requires resilience, adaptation, and inner strength.

Redemption and the Quest for Meaning: The Eden narrative does not end in despair; it hints at the potential for redemption and restoration. In the promise of Eve's offspring who will eventually overcome the serpent, there is a glimmer of hope. This quest for redemption becomes a recurring theme in religious traditions and cultural narratives, embodying humanity's ongoing search for wholeness, reconciliation, and connection with the divine. Redemption, in this sense, becomes a journey toward self-discovery and spiritual renewal—a journey that each of us undertakes in our own lives.

SETTING THE STAGE FOR OUR JOURNEY THROUGH EDEN'S STORY

In this book, we will explore the Garden of Eden, not just as an ancient narrative but as a timeless reflection of the human experience. Each chapter will delve into various aspects of the Eden story: the creation of paradise out of the Garden of the Universe, the symbolism of the forbidden tree, the choice and its consequences, the exile and human struggle, sex and pregnancy and childbirth, and finally, the universal quest for redemption. Together, these elements offer insights into our own lives, our challenges, and our search for connection and meaning.

The representation of Eve in the Adam and Eve narrative has often been scrutinised through the lens of feminist theory. Traditional interpretations frequently depict Eve as the archetypal sinner, whose actions lead to the Fall of humanity.

However, modern analyses dispute this perspective, arguing that these representations are culturally derived and symptomatic of wider societal biases against women.

For example, Arbel's study of the Greek Life of Adam and Eve (GLAE) shows a more nuanced depiction, asserting that Eve is not just the originator of sin but also embodies virtues that subvert this traditional narrative of guilt (Arbel, 2012).

Özsert's findings concur with this view, demonstrating that the Qur'an offers a more lenient account of Adam and Eve, and thereby diluting the misogynistic interpretations found in some biblical accounts (Özsert, 2023).

Furthermore, the balance of power and authority within the Eden narrative is crucial in understanding the relationship between Adam and Eve. In Milton's *Paradise Lost*, a convoluted set of gender roles is depicted, wherein Adam's apparent hegemonic stance is informed by Eve's desire for autonomy.

Woodford claims that Milton's vision of Eden as an egalitarian society is subverted by arbitrary divine command that constitutes Adam's sovereignty over Eve (Woodford, 2022). Paice further explores this tension in their gardening dispute, which illustrates a struggle for identity and agency within the parameters of roles (Paice, 2021).

The balance between domesticity and adventure, as illustrated in their contrasting gardening styles, mirrors the pervasive themes of freedom and constraint within.

The story of Adam and Eve also has psychological aspects that warrant consideration, especially tropes of individuation and Oedipus complex. Osman states that this narrative encompasses a psychodynamic struggle in which Adam and Eve's maturation leads to a crisis reflecting the difficulties of separation from parental figures (Osman, 2004).

Osman suggests that the Fall is not just a theological event, but also has deep psychological implications, resonating with the human experience of growth and loss. The psychodynamic perspective's implications also extend to religious practices, which attempt to deal with existential anxieties originating from original sin (Osman, 2000).

Beyond feminist and psychological interpretations, the literary aspects of the Eden narrative are replete with symbolism and thematic depth. The Garden of Eden itself is a metaphor for innocence and the ideal state of humanity before the Fall. Davis observes that "Edenic imagination" goes beyond mere nostalgia for a lost paradise; it is laden with a desire for belonging and transcendence in the fractured modern world (Davis, 2022).

This desire is depicted in artistic representations of Eden, such as Michelangelo's *The Creation of Adam*, which visually captures the tension between divine creation and human agency (Yi, 2023).

Moreover, an exploration of knowledge and its consequences is pivotal to the narrative. The Tree of Knowledge, a central part of the story, stands for the dichotomy between enlightenment and burden of choice. Wagner-Tsukamoto's rational choice interpretation suggests that Adam and Eve's eating of the fruit was not just an act of disobedience, but rather a complex interplay between self-interest and existential inquiry (Wagner-Tsukamoto, 2012).

This perspective allows for a reassessment of the moral implications of their actions—not as mere rebellion against divine authority, but rather an inquiry for understanding.

The contrasting expressions of sorrow between Adam and Eve following their expulsion from Eden further illuminate the complexities of their characters. Servin's analysis highlights how their lamentations reflect their distinct worldviews—Adam's spiritual anguish versus Eve's material grief—underscoring the gendered dimensions of their experiences (Servin, 2013).

This divergence in emotional expression not only enriches the narrative but also invites readers to consider the broader implications of gender roles in the context of loss and redemption.

As the narrative unfolds, the themes of exile and the search for redemption become increasingly prominent. The expulsion from Eden and into the vast expanse of the Garden of the Universe serves as a metaphor for the human condition, characterised by a longing for return to an ideal state.

The theological implications of this exile are profound, as they resonate with the broader narrative of salvation and the possibility of restoration. Al-Badarneh's examination of Milton's pro-feminist portrayal of Eve suggests that the narrative advocates for a reimagining of gender roles, positioning Eve as a figure of strength and agency rather than mere subservience (Al-Badarneh, 2014).

The interplay of freedom and authority in the Garden of Eden also raises questions about the nature of divine command and human autonomy. The tension between obedience to God and the exercise of free will is a central theme in both the Genesis account and Milton's retelling.

This dynamic is further complicated by the sociopolitical implications of the narrative, as it reflects the patriarchal structures that have historically governed interpretations of gender and power. Houwelingen's exploration of the male/female relationship in the context of 1 Timothy highlights how the Adam and Eve narrative has been utilized to reinforce gender hierarchies within religious communities (Houwelingen, 2019).

In conclusion, the story of Adam and Eve and the symbolism of Eden encapsulate a rich tapestry of themes that resonate across various disciplines. From feminist critiques to psychological analyses and literary interpretations, the narrative invites a multifaceted exploration of human nature, morality, and the quest for meaning.

The Garden of Eden, as both a literal and metaphorical space, serves as a poignant reminder of humanity's enduring struggle with innocence, knowledge, and the complexities of existence. As we reflect on this foundational myth, we are compelled to consider its implications for contemporary discussions surrounding gender, power, and the human condition.

As we journey through the Eden story, may we uncover new perspectives on our own lives. For just as Adam and Eve left Eden and embarked on a path toward discovery and growth in the Garden of the Universe, we too are on a journey shaped by choices, moments of loss, and the hope of finding redemption. In reflecting on Eden, we not only explore the roots of our shared spiritual heritage but also gain insight into our enduring quest for a life filled with purpose, peace, and connection.

CHAPTER 2

Purpose and Modern Relevance of the Story

A story passed down through the ages, Adam and Eve in the Garden of Eden is important to many cultures and religions. Often seen as a tale of defiance and downfall, it still resonates today: an admonition on the consequences of disobedience and need for moral rectitude.

This story is retold for the twenty-first century by exploring universal themes that resonate with contemporary matters and values: It becomes less about sin and fault-finding and more an exploration into curiosity, choices, collaboration, and self-discovery. The narrative explores these themes and provides a new reading of the old story, underlining personal growth and self-discovery.

The story of Adam and Eve can be interpreted as a love story—not just about two people falling in love, but also their journey to love themselves, seek knowledge, and bravely find truth. Rereading the text in this way allows for a range of interpretations and greater significance. Examining these motifs allows us to better appreciate the nuances and intricacies of love in Adam and Eve's story.

However, the Adam and Eve story does not merely define a relationship between people; it also includes self-discovery, pursuit of knowledge and truth, and the courage to learn facts hidden within oneself and in the universe.

The author wants us to interpret this story in many ways, casting light on some deeper shadows of its narrative. Understanding these ideas allows us to comprehend the complicated features of love in Adam and Eve's story.

This book explores how the Garden of Eden is portrayed as a paradise that is lost because of Adam and Eve's actions, analysing different scholarly viewpoints to uncover the deeper meanings and significance behind the Adam and Eve story.

The vivid depiction of Adam and Eve's time in paradise, their temptation, and eventual banishment serves to emphasise how fragile innocence is as well as the consequences of disobedience. Even though the story of the Garden of Eden is old, it still fascinates us with moral questions and dilemmas—engaging debates on topics such as good and evil, determinism, humanity's quest for knowledge, and salvation.

During the creation era, as folklore has it, lay an exquisite oasis—the Garden of Eden, said to be the handiwork of a deity who moulded Adam and Eve into existence. This holy sanctuary, abloom and abounding with life, was an equanimous realm—imperfect things did not exist in it. Wrongdoing, pain, and death had no place in such a state of impeccable existence.

This book delves into concepts of purity and conscience by bringing in the Tree of Knowledge of Good and Evil—with its enticing fruit—as a symbol of temptation, life choices on one's path to self-discovery, and moral responsibility. The tale shows in detail how giving into temptation leads to consequences when Adam and Eve fall prey to the serpent's inducement, thus incurring their famous loss of godly grace.

Now, their fate takes a turn and influences the fate of all humankind with a story of sin and hardship that unfolds soon after. It acts as the starting point of a saga that will linger throughout generations to come and forever change the trajectory of human development and civilisation.

The story of Eden has left an influence that extends far beyond its origins in the Bible by shaping beliefs on sin and salvation and offering insights into human nature. The narrative prompts reflection on the connection between humanity and divinity while exploring sociocultural themes. The depiction of Eden as an idyllic haven evokes a sense of yearning for a simpler past filled with innocence and harmony that resonates deeply across various faith traditions. The powerful symbolism of this speaks to a shared longing for an uncomplicated way of life that resonates with people worldwide.

Throughout history, the Garden of Eden has influenced culture with its inspiration depicted in paintings and literature. Its narrative has remained captivating with reinterpretations both past and present, while philosophers have delved into its deeper meanings, pondering its impact on human life and existence.

The tale of Eden goes beyond a mythical tale about how Adam and Eve's humanity began and offers deep insights into what it means to be human in this world we inhabit together. As we venture further into this storybook's journey, we uncover layers of significance that provoke contemplation and conversations about life's essence, our connections with the divine forces, and our timeless pursuit for a paradise long forgotten. The history of Eden is filled with a variety of themes and symbols that encourage us to reflect on where we come from and our dreams in a world that is constantly changing.

The biblical story of the Garden of Eden is one of the most influential narratives in human history, depicting the lives of Earth's first inhabitants: Adam and Eve. They dwell in a divine paradise, a lush and serene garden where their bond with God is unblemished and the beauty of nature envelops them. This garden is portrayed as a haven of abundance, peace, and perfection, free from pain or hardship, with every need effortlessly fulfilled.

In the book of Genesis from the Bible's Old Testament, the story of Creation and Adam and Eve's early days in the Garden of Eden marks a pivotal moment in humanity's relationship with learning and ethics. This is symbolised by two central trees: the Tree of Life and the Tree of Knowledge of Good and Evil, which represent the interplay of free will and moral decision-making.

God tells Adam and Eve to tend to the garden and gives them freedom with one rule: Do not eat the fruit from the Tree of Knowledge. Despite this commandment, a serpent tempts them to eat the fruit, resulting in what we now know as "the Fall." This act brings sin, pain, and death into existence and alters Adam and Eve's connection with God and the world forever.

Before the Fall, the story in Genesis 2:15 portrays Adam and Eve as caretakers of the garden with a "nurture and maintain" approach rather than a controlling one. Their innocence is tied to their role as stewards who care for nature rather than as stewards that assert dominance over it in this setting of abundance where everything is provided for them without scarcity or competition.

The tale of Eden has had an influence on global culture and philosophy beyond its religious importance by delving into themes such as human innocence—symbolically—and the pursuit of knowledge, along with the ethical dilemmas that follow it.

In Christian beliefs, Eden symbolises a state of grace lost through defiance, whereas in Judaism it reflects the challenge for humanity to harmonise divine laws with individual choice. In societies and traditions around the world, Eden symbolises a lost paradise, a perfect state of balance and a place that people long to go back to.

Eden's impact reaches beyond writings and has influenced various aspects of culture, like art and literature over many centuries. From John Milton's *Paradise Lost* poetry collection to Michelangelo's *Sistine Chapel* ceiling artwork, Eden's representation has moulded views on paradise and human nature as well as innocence.

Throughout eras as well as in today's world, the tale continues to spark conversations about our responsibility toward the environment and moral values and sheds light on human aspirations and motives at their core. Eden persists as a legend that prompts ongoing contemplation on the essence of humanity and the longing to find solace in a realm of purity and tranquillity that may be elusive.

In the Garden of Eden's storybook setting, Adam and Eve dwell in harmony with their surroundings owing to their pure innocence and lack of awareness of right and wrong. This allows them to embrace the garden without any doubts or fears and experience it naturally and instinctively. This state of connection resembles a form of human consciousness, a primitive yet innocent understanding that blurs the boundaries between oneself and the world around. They rely often on their instincts and trust rather than on logic or moral values.

The pure innocence of Adam and Eve could be seen as a connection with nature—a harmonious existence in which they only consume what is necessary and honour the natural equilibrium surrounding them. In contrast to modern humanity and the period after the Fall from Eden, Adam and Eve tend to see nature as something to exploit for resources as the first human couple to reside in coexistence with their surroundings.

Adam and Eve's purity is evident in the way they interact with each other. Lacking an understanding of right and wrong prevents them from feeling or passing judgment. They are described in Genesis 2:25 as "being naked without shame," which implies a sense of transparency, trust, and openness in their relationship. Their bond is free from self-awareness or selfish motives, enabling a genuine connection between them.

Adam and Eve symbolise a form of human connection that is free from doubts and tensions, and devoid of insecurities or discordant feelings that often plague relationships. Such profound closeness is not easily attained because it stems from a deep sense of completeness unaffected by moral dilemmas or conflicts. Their bond mirrors the coexistence they enjoy with nature and underscores the unity they feel within themselves and toward each other.

OVERVIEW OF THEMES: CURIOSITY, AUTONOMY, AND CONSCIOUSNESS

This story of Adam and Eve touches on timeless themes. In reinterpreting it for a modern context, we will expand on several themes that resonate deeply in today's world:

Curiosity: Eve's curiosity is often portrayed as a flaw, yet curiosity is essential to growth and learning. Here, we will see it as a virtue—signifying a desire to fully engage with life, to understand, and to move beyond what is simply given. Eve's curiosity about the Tree of Knowledge is not just a desire to "know"; it is a longing to experience the world and herself in a fuller way. Curiosity drives both Adam and Eve toward transformation, urging them to question, to seek, and to grow.

Autonomy: The choice to eat from the Tree of Knowledge represents a profound act of autonomy. It is not merely about disobedience; it is a testament to the importance of free will and the courage to choose even when the outcome is uncertain. Autonomy in this story symbolises the right—and the responsibility—to pursue one's truth, even at a cost. It is a theme that resonates with the modern search for individuality, self-determination, and authenticity.

Consciousness: The knowledge of good and evil marks Adam and Eve's entry into a more complex awareness. They gain a deeper understanding of themselves and the world around them, moving from a state of innocence to one of moral and personal consciousness. This awakening to duality—good and evil, joy and suffering—requires them to confront vulnerability and choice. Consciousness here is both a gift and a challenge, inviting them to grow as moral beings in a world of both light and shadow.

PARTNERSHIP AND EQUALITY

In this interpretation, Adam and Eve's relationship is central to their journey. Rather than seeing Eve's role as one of seduction or guilt, we will explore how she and Adam are partners who grow and learn together. Their journey outside the garden is not only a consequence of choice but also a development of their partnership. Together, they navigate love, mutual respect, and the complexities of individuality within a shared life. Their story speaks to the strength that comes from embracing one another's strengths, choices, and flaws.

THE POWER OF CHOICE AND RESPONSIBILITY

This narrative explores the impact of choice and the weight of responsibility that follows. Adam and Eve's decision to eat the fruit becomes a metaphor for humanity's eternal quest for freedom and the understanding that every choice shapes the world we live in. Theirs is not a choice without consequences but a choice that leads to growth, self-accountability, and the acknowledgment that actions define not only individuals but their relationship to each other and the world.

THE QUEST FOR MEANING AND BELONGING

In Eden, Adam and Eve live in a state of blissful innocence, yet there is an underlying restlessness, a yearning for something more meaningful and self-determined. The act of reaching for knowledge represents a deep-seated human quest for meaning, identity, and purpose. Through this lens, the journey outside Eden is a journey toward true belonging, not in a world of perfect bliss but in one where they create meaning together and find strength in both beauty and hardship.

LOVE AS A TRANSFORMATIVE FORCE

At the core of Adam and Eve's story is the transformative power of love— not only in a romantic sense but as a journey of self-love, forgiveness, and acceptance. Their love grows as they face challenges, as they come to terms with themselves and each other in a world that is no longer perfect. This love is not static; it evolves, and it demands growth, resilience, and compassion.

THE ECOLOGICAL DIMENSION

Finally, the story of Eden can be seen as an ecological parable. Eden represents the natural world, abundant and harmonious, but also fragile. The act of taking from the forbidden tree symbolises the human tendency to push boundaries with nature, sometimes leading to unforeseen consequences. Adam and Eve's expulsion can be seen as a lesson in respecting natural limits and understanding the delicate balance of the ecosystems around us—a theme deeply relevant in the twenty-first century's environmental consciousness.

WHY THIS STORY MATTERS TODAY

The story of Adam and Eve resonates in today's world because it is, at its core, about becoming fully human. Their journey reflects the timeless experiences of curiosity, love, choice, and responsibility, embodying the very essence of what it means to grow and learn. In this modern retelling, we will see them not as fallen figures, but as pioneers of human experience—figures who embrace the courage to know, to choose, and to love in the face of life's unknowns.

For the first time, *"Adam and Eve in the Garden"* explores the emotional and psychological journey of these two iconic figures. Eve is not merely deceived; she is searching for meaning, for understanding beyond the limits of her world. Adam does not simply follow blindly; he wrestles with his devotion to Eve and his role in the unfolding drama of creation.

In *"Adam and Eve in the Garden: A 21st Century Love Story"*, Chukky Daniels breathes new life into the timeless narrative, reimagining the first man and woman not as distant figures of myth, but as two people deeply in love, navigating the wonders and challenges of their existence together.

With lyrical prose and thought-provoking insight, the author challenges readers to see this ancient tale in a new light. It is a story of love in its purest form: passionate, flawed, and enduring. This is more than a story of loss; it is a story of love, resilience, and the journey of two people as they face an uncertain future together. As they step beyond the gates of Eden, banished from their perfect home, they must build a new life, relying on nothing but their love and the lessons learned from their time in paradise.

Through this reinterpretation, the author invites readers to reflect on their own journeys of discovery, growth, and partnership. This story encourages us to see Adam and Eve not as symbols of failure, but as relatable figures whose choices, love, and resilience mirror the human quest for truth, love, and meaning.

CHAPTER 3

The Tree of Knowledge: Innocence, Temptation, and Free Will

SETTING THE SCENE—LIFE IN EDEN

The life of Adam and Eve in Eden is idyllic—a paradise stocked with everything they need. They are happy and involved; they soar with the land, the animals, and one another. Here, they have everything they need, and fear and worry do not exist. They cannot feel shame or self-doubt, nor can they bear the weight of responsibility. They have a simple life in touch with nature.

In this state of innocence, Adam and Eve are close to the source of life itself, feeling connected not only to each other but also to a higher force that watches over them. They have no experience of harm or distrust, and in their minds, Eden is a place of perfect goodness.

HARMONY, TRUST, AND BOUNDARIES IN EDEN

In the paradisiacal Garden of Eden, Adam and Eve live in harmony until the serpent's temptation leads them to eat the forbidden fruit. This act awakens their consciousness, transforming their sibling bond into a profound love and casting them into a world of mortality and moral complexity. The narrative delves into their emotional journey from innocence to awareness, culminating in the birth of Cain and setting the stage for humanity's unfolding story.

As a storyteller and digital creator, I challenge conventional narratives with this book to offer fresh perspectives on enduring themes. Consequently, this novel invites readers to reconsider a foundational story through a contemporary lens, emphasising the human aspects of Adam and Eve's experiences.

In Eden, everything flows according to a natural order. Every creature has its place, and every tree, plant, and river serve a purpose. There is no conflict or competition. Adam and Eve are stewards of this paradise, charged with caring for its beauty, respecting its boundaries, and preserving its harmony.

The garden was not just a place; it was a world untouched by imperfection. Every flower bloomed eternally, every fruit ripened perfectly, and the air was alive with a peace Adam and Eve believed would never end. Yet, even in paradise, questions stirred in their hearts, questions that would change everything.

"Why are there two trees in the centre?" Eve asked one day. Her voice carried curiosity and the faintest trace of something else—an unspoken hunger for knowledge.

Adam shrugged. "The Creator warned us. The Tree of Life gives eternal life, and the other…" He trailed off. "We are not to touch or eat of the fruit of the Tree of Knowledge of Good and Evil."

Yes, despite this perfect environment, one boundary exists: they are forbidden to eat from the Tree of Knowledge of Good and Evil. The garden has many trees, each bearing abundant fruit, yet this one tree stands apart. It represents the limit of their understanding—a realm of knowledge that, so far, they are not ready to engage with. This boundary is a simple rule, and, as they live in innocence, they accept it without question.

THE GARDEN AS A MIRROR OF INNOCENCE

Eden, in its lush abundance, is not just a physical paradise but a mirror of Adam and Eve's state of mind. In their innocence, they only see what is good and harmonious. Just as the animals are unafraid of them and the trees give freely, Adam and Eve live in a world without inner conflict, untouched by the duality of good and evil.

This innocence means they have not yet experienced shame, guilt, or self-awareness. They are unaware of the complexities that lie within themselves. In Eden, they simply exist in the present moment, with no need for deeper questions or reflection. It is a life without ambiguity—a world where things simply exist.

EVE'S CURIOSITY AND DESIRE FOR UNDERSTANDING

As time passes, however, Eve continues to wonder about the world beyond the boundaries of Eden. Though she loves the garden, she feels a stirring of curiosity about herself and the world around her. What does it mean to know good and evil? Why is the Tree of Knowledge forbidden? These questions do not arise out of discontent; rather, they are a natural response to the complexity and beauty she sees in the world.

Eve's curiosity is subtle at first, like a gentle whisper in her mind. She does not act on it, but it grows within her, becoming a question that she can't fully answer. This curiosity does not take away from her happiness in Eden, but it adds a layer of wonder and intrigue. Eve's inquisitive nature marks the beginning of her journey toward self-awareness—a journey that will bring both beauty and complexity into her life.

Adam, however, is happy with the way Eden is. He likes the garden's predictability and the tranquil life with Eve. Though the forbidden tree exists, he does not feel a nagging urge toward it, nor does he see any reason for questioning the boundary that has been set up around it. While Adam and Eve are very much together, there is already a subtle difference in how they see things. Eve's curiosity starts to affect her perception of the world, whereas Adam is grounded in contentment and the present.

FORESHADOWING THE CHANGE TO COME

In this phase of their lives, Eden symbolises completeness and purity. Adam and Eve solely grasp the concept of good, remaining oblivious to their duality. Their life was simple, but it also meant that they were limited in knowledge about themselves and the world around them. Eve's curiosity suggests a wish for deeper knowledge—to know herself, and the world beneath its perfect surface.

This tension between contentment and curiosity, between innocence and the desire for knowledge, foreshadows the change that will come. Eve's questions are essentially the beginning of a journey that will take them outside Eden and face-to-face with all that it means to be human.

In the story of Adam and Eve, the Tree of Knowledge of Good and Evil is one of the most central motifs that is introduced. Together with the Tree of Life, this tree becomes central in our perceiving how innocence, temptation, and moral choice interrelate within the Garden of Eden.

The moment Adam and Eve learn about good and evil, they lose their innocence, and there is a shift from being one with everything to seeing everything as separate and different. They now see themselves as individuals, judge their nakedness, cover it, and fear being judged. With this new awareness comes shame and alienation, shattering the harmony within themselves, between one another, and in the rest of nature they once enjoyed.

THE SYMBOLISM OF THE TREE OF KNOWLEDGE

The Tree of Knowledge is deeply symbolic in the Eden story, signifying divine wisdom, moral perception, and God's limitations. Among the many fruitful trees that provide sustenance and amusement within this paradise, the Tree of Knowledge stands apart; it represents choosing freely between obedience to God versus independence. The tree's very presence brings a crucial element to human existence: free will.

In the story, the rule about the Tree of Knowledge was precise: "You may surely eat of every tree of the Garden, but of the Tree of Knowledge of Good and Evil, you shall not eat, for in the day that you eat of it you shall surely die." This command set the boundaries of Adam and Eve's freedom, allowing space for choice within their relationship with God.

The Tree of Life, on the other hand, represents a pure, never-dying life, free from human yearning and moral ambivalence. If the Tree of Knowledge is an awakening, the Tree of Life is a continuance, a gift of life from which no choice was necessary. In concert, these trees provide a tension: One promises everlasting life—the Tree of Life, the other, deep knowledge—the Tree of Knowledge of Good and Evil.

INNOCENT STATE OF ADAM AND EVE BEFORE THE FALL

Before coming across the Tree of Knowledge and gaining wisdom from it, Adam and Eve lived in a state of innocence where they were unaware of their nakedness and felt no shame about it. This reflected a genuine and unspoiled connection with both them and God. Their innocence symbolised a coexistence devoid of fear, remorse, or embarrassment. Just the delightful feeling of being connected with their Creator and the marvels of the universe.

Adam and Eve live each day surrounded by the beauty of the garden as they connect with nature in a respectful way. They revel in the act of creation and freedom from the weight of sin or ethical quandaries. Their purity symbolises an era when mankind was unaware of the complexities of morality. A time when life was straightforward and satisfying.

The tranquillity of the garden is disturbed when the serpent arrives in all its glory, surpassing all other creatures in wit and charm. The serpent sows seeds of doubt in Eve's mind by challenging God's directive with words and artful arguments.

With cunning and eloquence, the serpent challenges the command given by God, suggesting that the fruit of the Tree of Knowledge holds a secret power—a divine insight that would elevate them. "Did God say, 'You shall not eat of any tree in the garden'?" the serpent questions, introducing doubt into Eve's mind and encouraging her to consider the implications of disobedience.

In a modern, twenty-first-century reinterpretation of the encounter between Eve and the serpent, we might imagine the story unfolding in a way that resonates with contemporary themes like autonomy, curiosity, and the complexity of choice.

Eve is an inquisitive, intelligent figure who enjoys exploring and understanding her world. She's thoughtful, reflective, and increasingly curious about the boundaries around her and Adam's life in Eden. Adam, too, shares her curiosity but tends to follow established rules, comfortable in the predictable safety of their existence. They live in a beautiful, peaceful environment—a garden paradise where everything seems perfect, but where certain questions about freedom, choice, and self-awareness linger beneath the surface.

The garden was not just a place; it was a world untouched by imperfection. Every flower bloomed eternally, every fruit ripened perfectly, and the air was alive with a peace Adam and Eve believed would never end. Yet, even in paradise, questions stirred in their hearts, questions that would change everything.

"Why are there two trees in the centre?" Eve asked one day. Her voice carried curiosity and the faintest trace of something else—an unspoken hunger for knowledge.

Adam shrugged. "The Creator warned us. The Tree of Life gives eternal life, and the other…" He trailed off. "But…we are not to touch the Tree of Knowledge of Good and Evil."

Eve's eyes lingered on the forbidden tree, its fruit gleaming in the sunlight.

As Eve contemplates the beauty of Eden and the mystery of the forbidden tree, her curiosity grows. She has never questioned the rules before, but the very existence of a tree she cannot touch makes her wonder: Why would something so beautiful be out of reach? What could be so significant about knowledge that it requires a boundary? These questions become part of her, shaping her perspective in subtle ways. She begins to feel a gentle restlessness, a desire to understand more deeply.

Eve's eyes lingered on the forbidden tree, its fruit gleaming in the sunlight. One day, Eve encounters the serpent, who is sharp, persuasive, and skilled in navigating questions that others might avoid. The serpent, seeing Eve's intelligence and curiosity, engages her in a conversation, knowing she is already wondering about the boundaries set around her. Instead of a direct temptation, the serpent introduces her to the power of questioning, gently encouraging her to think about the forbidden fruit as a symbol of untapped potential.

Eve's encounter with the serpent is not a simple temptation. It is a moment of deep conflict. The serpent asks her to reconsider everything she's known and introduces an idea that had never occurred to her: that maybe knowledge is not inherently dangerous. Maybe it's the key to becoming more than what she currently is.

The temptation is not just about eating the fruit, it's about daring to challenge boundaries, questioning the very essence of what it means to obey and be free. This internal struggle is pivotal for Eve as she realizes that knowledge will come at a cost.

Here is a dialogue capturing the tension and curiosity as the Serpent engages Eve, explaining the Tree of Knowledge and subtly planting seeds of doubt about God's command:

"Why don't you taste the fruit of this tree?" the serpent asks her. "Are you not curious? Do you not wish to see the world through the lens of true understanding?

Eve hesitates, but her curiosity has already been awakened. "But we are not allowed," she says. "This is the one rule we must follow. The fruit of this tree is forbidden."

Serpent: "Eve, have you ever thought about why you are not allowed to taste this fruit? A fruit that could give you more understanding and a new perspective. Don't you wonder what else there is to see, to know?"

Eve listens, considering the serpent's words, and for the first time, feels a kind of autonomy stir within her. The idea of choosing for herself, of gaining wisdom that is not simply handed down to her, appeals deeply. The serpent does not compel her; rather, it presents an opportunity to explore new possibilities, guiding her towards a deeper understanding of her own autonomy.

Her gaze shifts from the fruit to the lush beauty of the garden around her, to the streams and trees, the flowers and creatures, all vibrant and innocent. This is the only forbidden thing in all of creation—the one barrier between her and a world she does not yet fully comprehend.

The serpent regards her with a knowing look. "Why would such knowledge be forbidden? Knowledge itself cannot be evil. It is only by knowing that we can truly understand the beauty and complexity of the world around us. This fruit will open your eyes, and you will see the world in its fullness."

Eve: [Gazing up at the Tree of Knowledge] This tree is unlike any other. Its fruit looks… different. We have been told never to eat it, nor to touch it. It is forbidden.

Serpent: [Coiling gracefully around a branch] Forbidden? Why should a fruit so beautiful, so ripe, be forbidden to you? Have you ever wondered, Eve, why such a rule was given?

Eve: God told us that if we eat from this tree, we will surely die. So, we stay away from it.

Serpent: [Pausing thoughtfully] Die? Is that what you honestly believe? Look around you, Eve. This garden is filled with life, with abundance. I see no shadow of death here.

Eve: But… I trust God. He created me, created this place. He knows what is best for me. If He says this fruit will bring death, I believe Him.

Serpent: [Softly, with a hint of persuasion] It's not death as you imagine, Eve. Perhaps it is something else. [pauses] Do you know what makes this tree special? Why is it called the Tree of Knowledge?

Eve: No. I do not know. It is simply the Tree of Knowledge of Good and Evil.

Serpent: [Nods knowingly] Precisely. The Tree of Knowledge of Good and Evil. Tell me, do you know what it means to understand good… and evil?

Eve: [Hesitates] No. I only know about "good," because everything here is good. What more do I need?

Serpent: Ah, but that is just it. You have not known the fullness of life—its wonders and its mysteries. Imagine knowing as God knows, seeing beyond what is good to what is hidden and unknown. Eating the fruit from this tree would open your eyes, Eve.

Eve: [Curiosity begins to stir in her] Open my eyes? How? About what?

Serpent: About knowledge, Eve. About wisdom beyond your dreams. To understand both light and shadow, good and evil, and to see as He sees. This fruit holds the key to your true self, to wisdom, to choice. [pauses, observing her reaction] Why should God keep that from you?

Eve: [Furrows her brow] But if I eat it, I will die. That is what He told me.

Serpent: [Chuckles softly] Die? Or… become more? God knows that when you eat of this fruit, you will be like Him, knowing both good and evil. Perhaps that is why He warned you, Eve—not because it would bring death, but because it would bring something He wishes to keep for Himself.

Eve: [Eyes the fruit more closely] To be like Him… to know as He knows… [pauses, her voice filled with a mix of wonder and apprehension] But… I do not want to disobey Him.

Serpent: Disobedience, or choice? How can you grow, how can you truly live, without making choices for yourself? [leans in] Perhaps God's only test is to see if you are bold enough, curious enough, to take what He has placed before you.

Eve: [Whispers to herself] To know… to see beyond this garden… [louder, still hesitant] But what if it changes everything?

Serpent: [Smoothly] Everything worth discovering changes us, Eve. Perhaps the only way to truly understand your purpose here is to take that first step. Take, and see. Taste, and know. The choice is yours alone.

The Serpent's words are laden with deception, subtly suggesting that eating from the tree will not lead to death but rather to enlightenment. "For God knows that when you eat of it, your eyes will be opened, and you will be like God, knowing good and evil." This insidious temptation highlights a critical theme: the struggle between divine authority and human autonomy.

At this moment, the serpent's words have planted enough doubt and curiosity in Eve's mind. The Serpent's words tantalize, suggesting that consuming the fruit will "open their eyes" and make them be "like gods," knowing both good and evil. It is an understated prompt to critically evaluate authority and contemplate alternative possibilities. In this subtle, persuasive way, the Serpent plants a seed of curiosity, introducing the allure of the forbidden and making Eve question the limits imposed upon her.

As Eve stands before the Tree of Knowledge, her eyes fixed on the fruit that glistens in the sunlight. Her heart beats faster, stirred by the serpent's words still lingering in her mind like an echo: "You will not surely die… You will be like God, knowing good and evil." The promise of knowledge, of wisdom beyond her current understanding, is irresistible.

The serpent's words resonate deeply with Eve's own unspoken questions. She realizes that this desire to know is not just curiosity—it is a longing to understand herself, her world, and her purpose. The tree becomes a symbol of self-awareness, and her fear of disobedience is now matched by a powerful need to know.

In that pivotal moment, Eve stands before the Tree of Knowledge, grappling with the allure of wisdom and the command of God. The fruit appears enticing, desirable for gaining knowledge and wisdom. Caught in the web of temptation, she chooses to eat the fruit, an act that symbolizes both the will to disobey and the exercise of free will. The forbidden fruit glowed as if lit from within, and in that moment, desire outweighed obedience.

Eve's hand trembles as she reaches for the fruit. Hesitating, she pulls her hand back, glancing around as if expecting to see God Himself watching. The air seems to grow thick, the garden itself holding its breath in suspense. Then, with a steady breath, she steps closer to a particular fruit. Her fingers brush against the fruit's smooth surface, cool and firm beneath her touch. The serpent's voice lingers in her mind, urging her forward, promising enlightenment, freedom. She closes her hand around the fruit, feeling a surge of anticipation.

Finally, with one deliberate motion, she plucks the fruit from the tree. Her hands tremble slightly as she brings the fruit to her lips. With one bite, a flood of sensations overwhelms her—both wonder and fear, awe, and realization, mingling within her as her eyes seem to open wider than before. Colors deepen; sounds sharpen; the world around her takes on new shades she had not noticed. But there is also a strange new sensation—a stirring within, an awareness of herself, of her vulnerability, of something lost that she cannot quite name.

Eve's Choice and the Invitation to Adam

As the taste of the fruit lingers, Eve feels a shift in her perception. She becomes aware of herself in a way she never has before. The world around her appears both brighter and more complex, filled with layers she had never noticed. For the first time, she feels both awe and vulnerability, the recognition that beauty and imperfection coexist.

She feels more aware—of herself, of the garden, of the dynamics around her. She sees things in layers, perceiving complexity and subtlety in ways that had previously eluded her. With this new awareness, however, comes a sense of vulnerability and accountability. She feels the weight of her choice but also the thrill of having acted of her own free will.

Eve's decision is not simply about defying a rule. It's about stepping into her own curiosity and desire for understanding. She realizes that knowledge—though possibly challenging—could bring her closer to who she truly is and could help her and Adam grow together in ways they have not yet considered.

After tasting the fruit, Eve approaches Adam thoughtfully, aware that he may not immediately understand why she took this step. When Eve told Adam of her encounter with the serpent, her voice trembled with a mixture of excitement and trepidation.

Eve says, "Adam, I did something today that changed me. I chose to eat from the tree—the one we were told to avoid. But I see things differently now. I feel more aware, more connected to myself and everything around us. It is as if I've discovered a part of me that I didn't know was there. The serpent said I would not die—and look at me, Adam. I am still alive! I see more now. I feel... more aware."

Adam looks at her, surprised and hesitant. He's uneasy about breaking rules because he's content with the familiar. But Eve's newfound confidence and self-awareness intrigue him.

Adam's face darkens. "You spoke to the serpent? He is cunning and deceitful! But we were told it is forbidden, Eve. Isn't that enough reason to leave it alone? What if something terrible happens?"

"I understand. But nothing terrible has happened, Adam. I feel…alive, aware. I see you in a new way. This knowledge brings us closer, makes us more connected. We are more than we thought we were. Please, trust me. This is more than just obeying or disobeying. I feel like we're meant to think, to choose, to grow. Don't you want to see the world as it really is? This could help us understand each other and our surroundings better. It is not about rebellion—it's about becoming fully ourselves."

Eve looks away, arms crossed, frustration clouding her face and guilt flickering in her eyes. "I thought he lied, but the fruit…it did something to me. I wanted you to share it too."

Adam moves closer, speaking in a calm manner. "Eve, even when I do not understand, I see you. I see your strength, your love, your sacrifice." Then he takes her hands to comfort her and speak the words that had been resting in his heart…

Come, take my hand,

Let burdens cease,

Let hearts entwine

In love and peace.

Adam then turns toward the center of the garden where the forbidden tree stood, its fruit glistening in the sunlight. Without another word, he marches toward it, his mind swirling with fury and a determination to confront the creature that had led Eve astray.

The serpent was waiting, coiled elegantly on a low-hanging branch. Its eyes sparkled with cunning as Adam approached.

"You deceived her!" Adam roared. "You told her lies, and now we are cursed."

The serpent's voice was calm, almost amused. "Lies? Or truths you were too afraid to face? Your Creator placed the fruit here knowing you would one day desire it. I merely pointed her toward what was already in her heart."

"You dare speak to her?" Adam bellowed; fists clenched. "You have brought ruin to what was perfect."

The serpent tilted its head, its voice calm and soothing. "Ruin? Or awakening? Your Eve sees what she could not see before. She now sees the world clearly."

Adam's jaw tightened. "And at what cost? She has doomed us all to death."

The serpent chuckled softly. "Death is not the end, Adam. Knowledge is Life. By eating, she has stepped into a higher plane of existence. Do you love her so little that you would leave her to bear this burden alone?"

Adam's anger faltered. The serpent's words gnawed at his mind. Did he love her so little? Could he abandon her to face this new awareness by herself?

"Eat, Adam," the serpent said, its voice almost a whisper. "Eat, and you will see as she sees. You will understand as she understands. Together, you will be as one, bound not by ignorance but by truth."

Adam walks back to Eve; and with trembling hands, he reaches for Eve's outstretched hand with the fruit, takes the fruit from her hand and takes a bite. He, too, feels the change immediately—the opening of his mind, the acute awareness of his vulnerabilities, and a sudden depth to everything he once took for granted.

The world shifted. The vibrant colors of the garden dimmed. A weight they could not name settled on their shoulders, and for the first time, they see each other's nakedness…they knew shame. The serpent watched in silence as Adam bit into the fruit, sealing their fate.

The sweetness of the fruit belied the weight that immediately descended upon him. His eyes widened as the garden seemed to darken, its perfection now tinged with shadows he had never noticed before.

Eve approached him, her hand slipped into his. They were no longer innocent, but they were together. Eve's perspective resonates with something in Adam, though he feels uncertain and nervous. He trusts her, though, and he trusts the strength of their partnership. He realizes that if Eve's choice brought her to a new awareness, it might do the same for him—and he doesn't want to be left behind in understanding this new awareness.

This choice marks a profound turning point in the narrative, as it signifies not just a physical act of disobedience but a spiritual rebellion against the divine order. By choosing to eat from the tree, Adam and Eve assert their independence, stepping into a new reality where knowledge comes with consequences.

The pivotal moment came when Eve, tempted by the promise of wisdom, reached out to take the fruit. In this act, she exercises her free will, choosing to explore beyond the bounds set for her. This choice—simple yet world-altering—signifies humanity's first step into moral autonomy. Adam joins her, sharing in her decision; and in this moment of disobedience, they step into the realm of experience and consequence.

The act of consuming the fruit is more than a mere breaking of a rule; it is a profound exercise of free will that forever alters the bond between humanity and the divine. They are no longer passive beings but individuals with the power of choice, marking a shift in the human condition.

The immediate aftermath of this choice is a sudden, shocking awareness. Their eyes are opened, as the serpent promised. But the knowledge they gain brings not divine power but vulnerability. They become aware of their nakedness, a realization that evokes shame and a desire to hide. For the first time, they cover themselves, breaking from their previous innocence. This new awareness signifies a loss of harmony with themselves, with each other, and with God. The simplicity and purity of Eden is replaced by complexity, self-consciousness, and the profound feeling of separation.

The themes of choice and freedom will resonate deeply within the Eden narrative. Humanity is granted the ability to choose, reflecting God's respect for human agency. This act of choice is essential for the development of moral consciousness; it is through making choices—right and wrong—that humanity learns, grows, and ultimately seeks redemption.

The consequences of Adam and Eve's choice echo throughout history, shaping theological interpretations across various traditions. For many, the Eden narrative serves as a cautionary tale about the implications of free will and the importance of adhering to divine guidance.

The act of eating the fruit signifies a deeper transformation: the loss of innocence and the introduction of moral complexity. The knowledge of good and evil brings with it the burden of choice, guilt, and the awareness of their separation from God.

Theological interpretations of this moment vary, but many see it as essential to understanding free will and humanity's unique role in creation. Free will, in this context, is seen as a divine gift, allowing humans to choose rather than follow blindly. In Christianity, the act is often seen as the "original sin," introducing the need for salvation. Jewish interpretations sometimes focus on the complexity of good and evil, suggesting that moral understanding is a natural part of human maturity.

Islamic tradition often interprets the story as a reminder of human frailty and the importance of repentance, viewing Adam and Eve's actions as part of a divine plan rather than an irreversible fall. Across these perspectives, the Eden story presents free will as a path to wisdom and responsibility, with the Tree of Knowledge serving as both an invitation and a challenge.

Philosophically, the Tree of Knowledge story raises enduring questions about the nature of choice, the pursuit of wisdom, and the human condition. Augustine, a prominent thinker in Christian theology, viewed the Fall as essential to human consciousness, a step from innocence into self-awareness and moral responsibility. He saw humanity's journey as one of understanding the consequences of freedom, with the fall as a necessary part of growth.

HARMONY, TRUST, AND BOUNDARIES IN EDEN

Rather than simply portraying Eve as weak for being tempted, we could see her grappling with the deeper desire for knowledge, autonomy, and a fuller existence. The serpent can be seen not just as a villain, but as an agent of change, pushing Eve to question her limitations. In modern terms, it might represent the voice of inner curiosity, the one that challenges convention and pushes for transformation.

The "fruit" could be linked to the symbol of "forbidden knowledge" or the "awakening of self-awareness." This is a pivotal moment in the story when Eve chooses to embrace both the risk and the potential for deeper understanding, leading to growth, but not without consequence.

In this retelling, Eve is less of a seductress or "temptress" and more of an empowered individual who chooses to seek knowledge. Her decision is not impulsive; it is driven by a desire for growth, understanding, and partnership. Rather than passively accepting rules, she considers her choices and takes responsibility for them, reshaping the traditional narrative of blame. Adam, too, joins her not because he is pressured, but because he is inspired by her bravery and her vision of what they can become together.

Modern perspectives often interpret the Tree of Knowledge as a symbol of moral freedom, with the choice to eat the fruit reflecting the tension between innocence and maturity, obedience and exploration. Some see it as humanity's first step toward enlightenment, a journey that involves both struggle and understanding.

The Tree of Knowledge, in the end, represents the human journey itself—a path marked by choices, mistakes, growth, and the pursuit of wisdom. It is a symbol of our capacity to seek and to understand, yet it also reminds us of the weight of knowledge and the responsibility that comes with it.

As we reflect on this story, we may ask ourselves: How does knowledge shape our lives, and what responsibilities come with the insights we gain? The story of Eden invites us to ponder not only where we came from but also where we are going, urging us to reflect on the choices that define us.

The serpent's decision to tempt Eve instead of Adam has intrigued readers and scholars for centuries, and while the Bible does not explicitly explain the serpent's reasoning, there are several interpretations that offer insights into why Eve might have been approached first:

Curiosity and Open-Mindedness: Eve may have represented a spirit of curiosity and openness, as she was newer to the world and potentially more inquisitive about her surroundings. The serpent might have seen this curiosity as a quality that could lead her to question God's command more easily.

Influence in the Relationship: In ancient storytelling, women were often viewed as strong influences in relational dynamics. By convincing Eve to eat the fruit first, the serpent could have assumed she might then share it with Adam, making her the perfect starting point to introduce doubt and disobedience into humanity.

Symbolic Representation of Humanity's Vulnerability: Some interpretations suggest that Eve represents a more vulnerable aspect of humanity, one more open to questioning and exploring the unknown. The serpent might have chosen her because of this symbolic openness, seeing an opportunity to exploit human curiosity and desire.

Testing the Power of Persuasion: The serpent may have simply seen Eve as more susceptible to persuasion, with her role and proximity to Adam offering a way to extend the temptation indirectly to him. By persuading Eve, the serpent would essentially be evaluating the strength of human commitment to God's command.

Challenge to God's Order: Another interpretation is that the serpent's temptation was a subversive act against the order God established in creation. Since Eve was created as Adam's companion, approaching her could have been an attempt to disrupt the harmony and order God had set, introducing division and distrust within humanity.

Each of these perspectives sheds light on why the serpent might have seen Eve as a key to humanity's Fall, whether for her perceived openness, her relational influence, or what she symbolised. The story highlights the human qualities of curiosity, vulnerability, and the exercise of free will, setting the stage for the larger themes of knowledge, choice, and consequence that unfold in the Eden narrative.

Their story, then, becomes a parable of autonomy, partnership, and the courage to embrace life's complexities. It highlights the idea that growth often involves leaving comfort zones, questioning given structures, and taking ownership of one's actions—even when the consequences are unknown. In this version, Eve's act is not one of defiance for its own sake but a symbol of humanity's enduring quest for knowledge, self-awareness, and authentic connection.

CHAPTER 4:
The Serpent: A Catalyst for Change

In chapter 4, we explore the immediate and lasting consequences of Adam and Eve's choice, focusing on the exile from Eden and its profound significance for humanity. This chapter will delve into the sorrow of separation, the new challenges they face outside paradise, and the theological and symbolic meanings of exile. It also considers humanity's enduring quest to reconcile with the divine and regain a lost sense of harmony.

THE ROLE OF ENVY IN THIS SAGA

Envy is a subtle but intriguing undercurrent in the story of Adam and Eve, though it is not explicitly named. Examining the roles of each character, especially the serpent, allows us to see how envy might have influenced the actions and choices that ultimately led to the Fall from Eden.

> **The Serpent's Envy**: In traditional interpretations, the serpent is often viewed as a symbol of Satan or as an agent of chaos who seeks to disrupt God's creation. One possible motivation for the serpent's actions could be envy of humanity's special relationship with God. Adam and Eve were created in God's image and given dominion over all living things, a status that sets them apart in the natural order. If the serpent or Satan felt envious of this divine connection or privileged position, tempting Eve to disobey God would be a way to undermine that special relationship. The serpent suggests to Eve that by eating the fruit, she could "be like God," hinting that Eve too could desire what God alone possesses: supreme knowledge and autonomy.

Eve's Envy of Divine Knowledge: The serpent's tempting words play on an element of envy that may have been brewing within Eve herself—a desire for wisdom and power that she does not possess. When the serpent says that eating the forbidden fruit would make her be "like God, knowing good and evil," it introduces the possibility of a godlike status. Eve's choice to eat the fruit reflects her desire to possess what she perceives as a superior kind of knowledge and power. Her actions suggest an envious yearning for qualities attributed to God, which she perhaps believes would complete or perfect her.

Adam's Envy or Desire to Match Eve: Adam's choice to eat the fruit, despite knowing God's command, could also hint at a form of envy or desire to remain on an equal level with Eve. Seeing that Eve has eaten the fruit, Adam might feel compelled to do the same—whether out of love, curiosity, or even a desire not to be left behind in this new awareness. This act reflects a complex mix of emotions, potentially including envy of the new experience Eve has embraced, despite its risks.

The Consequences of Envy: In broader theological interpretations, the entire Fall can be seen as humanity's envy of divine wisdom and autonomy, leading them to overstep their intended role. This choice disrupts the harmony of Eden and distances humanity from God. Envy, therefore, leads to a loss of innocence, separation from the divine, and the introduction of suffering into the world. In this sense, envy is portrayed as a destructive force that disrupts harmony and brings about unintended consequences.

Envy and the Human Condition: The story of Adam and Eve symbolically highlights one constant of humanity—wanting what others have, desiring that which is beyond our grasp. Essentially, it's a warning tale about envy and the dangers of crossing limits or lines to obtain things we do not possess.

Thus, envy is intricately woven into the story as a force that drives and triggers the Fall. It symbolises how humans have always been torn between being content with what they have and wanting more—something that impacts individuals as well as their world.

Eve's encounter with the serpent is not a simple temptation. It is a moment of deep conflict. The serpent asks her to reconsider everything she has known and introduces an idea that had never occurred to her: that maybe knowledge is not inherently dangerous. Maybe it is the key to becoming more than what she currently is.

The temptation is not just about eating the fruit—it's about daring to challenge boundaries, questioning the very essence of what it means to obey and be free. This internal struggle is pivotal for Eve as she realises that knowledge will come at a cost.

Desire for Connection: Eve and Adam shared a deep bond, the first and only two people in a mysterious and vast world known as the Garden of Eden. This closeness meant that she wanted Adam to experience what she had just discovered. Whatever the fruit brought—wisdom, knowledge, or even the potential for consequences—Eve might have felt that she did not want to face it alone.

Curiosity and Enthusiasm: After tasting the fruit, Eve might have felt a rush of new understanding and awareness, however confusing or overwhelming. This could have sparked an eagerness to share that experience with Adam, wanting him to feel the same sense of insight, even if it came with uncertainty.

Trust in the Serpent's Words: The serpent's words had planted the idea in Eve's mind that eating the fruit would make her "like God, knowing good and evil." She may have genuinely believed this new knowledge was something powerful and beneficial, something she wanted Adam to share in. If she felt that the serpent's promise of wisdom was being fulfilled in her own mind, she might have seen it as something too valuable for Adam to miss.

A Sense of Defiance or Liberation: By eating the fruit, Eve had already crossed a boundary. In that moment, sharing it with Adam might have felt like a natural next step—a way to solidify her choice and the sense of independence or self-direction she was exploring. She may have wanted Adam to join her in that newfound independence, for better or worse.

Desire to Alleviate Guilt or Responsibility: Eve may have sensed, on some level, that her action was a transgression. Inviting Adam to share the fruit could have been a way of lessening her own sense of guilt or responsibility. By sharing it, she was not alone in her choice.

Fear of Change Without Him: With her new awareness, Eve might have sensed that she was changed, somehow separate from her former self—and by extension, from Adam. Offering him the fruit might have been an attempt to restore their unity and make sure that whatever came next, they would face it together.

In the end, Eve's decision to share the fruit could be seen as a mixture of love, curiosity, and a desire for companionship in the face of the unknown. It underscores the human longing for connection and understanding, even when faced with choices that carry heavy consequences.

In that instant, the world shifts irreversibly. They look at each other with new eyes, suddenly aware of their own nakedness, their vulnerability, and a strange, penetrating feeling of shame. They reach for leaves to cover themselves, realising they are exposed in ways they never were before. The garden, once a place of pure innocence, now feels different—still beautiful, but shadowed by the weight of knowledge. They sense the gravity of their choice, the world around them holding its breath, as though all of creation has been changed in that single, shared act of disobedience.

The first sin in Eden raises questions about the origins of evil and humanity's inclination toward disobedience. The act of disobedience in the Garden of Eden marks the beginning of a profound transformation in the human experience. This chapter delves into the consequences of Adam and Eve's choices, exploring the themes of shame, judgment, and the lasting impact of the Fall.

Following the fateful decision to eat the forbidden fruit, Adam and Eve's perception of themselves and their relationship with God undergoes a drastic change. The once peaceful and harmonious environment of the Garden is now clouded by the weight of their actions. The immediate consequence of their disobedience is the realisation of their nakedness, which leads to a sense of vulnerability and shame.

As Adam and Eve attempt to navigate their new reality, the Creator seeks them out. "Where are you?" God asks a question that resonates with profound significance. It is not merely a physical inquiry but an exploration of their spiritual state. Adam responds, acknowledging their shame and fear, stating, "I heard the sound of you in the Garden, and I was afraid, because I was naked, and I hid myself."

In an instinctive response, they attempt to cover themselves with fig leaves, a symbolic gesture that reflects their new awareness of sin and the need to hide from God. The innocence that characterised their existence has been shattered, replaced by an unsettling consciousness of self.

God's response is layered with a mixture of sadness and justice. He confronts Adam and Eve about their disobedience, asking, "Have you eaten of the tree of which I commanded you not to eat?" The act of questioning serves not only to reveal the gravity of their actions but also to highlight the breakdown in their relationship with the divine.

The consequences of their choice unfold as God pronounces judgment. For Eve, the punishment entails increased pain in childbirth and a complex relationship with her husband. For Adam, the ground is cursed because of his actions, and he will toil for his sustenance. The divine pronouncement encapsulates the depth of the rupture in their existence, as the idyllic harmony of Eden gives way to struggle and strife.

Adam was destined to leave paradise for the world beyond (Earth?) as part of a plan. The Garden of Eden is now quiet and sombre as Adam and Eve stand together, absorbing the weight of God's words. Adam and Eve's sudden awareness of their nakedness reflects their new self-consciousness and loss of innocence after gaining knowledge.

Eve: [Voice trembling as she turns to Adam] "Adam, what have we done? Everything has changed now. The garden, God's presence, all slipping away. I feel…so different. I did not know it would end like this. I just…I thought it would make us wise, as the serpent said."

Adam: [Heavy sigh] "I feel it too, Eve. The peace, the safety we knew—it is all gone." [Pauses, glancing at her] "We have lost so much because we wanted to know what was not meant for us." [Sighing, looking down] "I am sorry, Eve. I did not stop you from eating the fruit because I wanted it, too. But now everything has changed. We cannot go back to the way things were."

Eve: "It is so strange—I feel exposed, like I am seeing the world differently, but not in the way I thought I would. There is this feeling of shame, and a kind of fear that was not there before."

Adam: [Nodding] "Yes, I feel it, too. That innocence we had…it is gone. Now, we know what it means to be naked and vulnerable. To be… separated."

Eve: [Chokes back tears] "I wanted to be more, Adam. I thought…I thought it would bring us closer to Him, to understand, to see as He does. I never thought it would cost us everything."

Adam: [Gently] "I know." [Takes her hand] "But I chose to eat the fruit too. You did not do this alone. I could have said no—I should have. But I did not because the serpent convinced me too."

Eve: [Looks away] "But it was I who listened, who believed the serpent." [Shakes her head] "I thought…I thought I could handle the truth, the knowledge. I never dreamed it would bring pain or the shame from disobedience. I cannot undo it, Adam."

Adam: "Neither can I. But…" [Pauses] "We must live with it now. The land is no longer a gift freely given. God said I will have to toil, to labour against thorns and thistles. Everything that was once easy, flowing—now it will be hard."

Eve: "Do you think we will survive outside the garden? I am so afraid. And the pain… He said there would be pain." [Places a hand on her stomach, trembling]

Adam: [Puts his hand on her shoulder gently] "I do not know, Eve. But He also said we would work the ground for food, that we could still live. It will not be the same…we will not have everything given to us. We will have to struggle. But maybe…we can make something of it. Somehow."

Eve: [Whispers] "And I will bear children in pain. The joy of bringing life… now mixed with suffering." [Tears stream down her face] "I never imagined this kind of pain, Adam, even before it happened."

Adam: [Squeezes her hand] "I am so sorry, Eve. For both of us. But He also promised that life would continue—that we would still have each other." [Pauses] "I do not know what this world will be like outside the Garden, but I will not leave you to face it alone."

Eve: [Softly, with a small, sad smile] "Thank you, Adam. I am afraid…but somehow knowing we will face it together gives me strength. Maybe this is what it means to be truly human—to live with the weight of our choices, and to keep going."

Adam: [Nods] "Yes, we must go on. Though it feels like the end of paradise, it is a beginning too. We will find our way, even if it is with broken hearts." [Looks at her earnestly] "And perhaps someday…maybe He will forgive us."

Eve: [Nods, finding a glimmer of hope in his words] "Yes. Maybe there is a way back to Him, even if it is not the same. We will carry His words with us, Adam. And hopefully, through our children, through everything we do from now on, we can find some kind of redemption."

Adam: [Resolute] "We will make a life, Eve. For us and for those who come after us. We have lost Eden, but we have not lost each other…or our hope. We will learn to live with this knowledge. And somehow, we will find a way to endure. Together."

Eve: [Tearfully] "I miss the peace we had here, Adam. That feeling that everything was whole. I did not realise how precious it was until it was gone."

Adam: "Neither did I. I feel like this loss is inside me now, like a shadow. But maybe we can learn to live with it, somehow, outside the garden."

Eve: [Looking up, determined] "We have each other. And we can still turn to Him, even though we have fallen. He did not abandon us completely. I think He will be with us, somehow…even in our sorrow."

Adam: "Yes. We will do our best to be faithful, even with this knowledge, this weight. And maybe…someday, we will understand why He did this. Why we were allowed to choose, and why we're being cast out."

Eve: "I hope you are right." [Pauses, looking around one last time at the garden] "Let us go, Adam. The garden will live on without us…but we must learn to live on without it."

Adam: [Sighs, nodding resolutely] "Yes. Together."

The weight of their choice hung heavy in the air, yet for a brief moment, they sought refuge in each other. Twilight had begun to settle over the garden, painting the sky in hues of amber and violet. The soft whisper of the breeze carried the distant songs of birds, as if Eden itself was offering them a final farewell.

By the edge of a familiar stream, Adam and Eve stood together, the water lapping gently at their feet. Eve dipped her fingers into the cool stream, tracing ripples along its glassy surface. Adam watched her, his heart tightening at the thought of what was to come.

She turned to him then, her eyes reflecting both sorrow and love. "No matter where we go," she whispered, "we go together."

Adam reached for her hand, drawing her close. "Even in exile, even in the unknown, I will love you." His voice was steady, a vow that would stand against time itself.

Eve rested her head against his chest, listening to the steady rhythm of his heartbeat. For a moment, there was no fear, no regret, only the warmth of his embrace. He pressed a kiss on her forehead and allowed it to linger there as if trying to capture the essence of the garden in one final touch.

As the first stars flickered to life above them, they held each other, bound not by paradise but by love itself. Soon, they would walk into an unfamiliar world; and in that moment, beneath the heavens that still bore witness to their love, they were whole.

And as the gates of Eden loomed before them, glowing with divine fire, they stepped forward—not as two lost souls, but as one.

Their relationship represents the genesis from which all of humanity was born.

Adam and Eve turn away, leaving the garden hand in hand, their footsteps marking the beginning of a new, unknown path.

The Creator's voice thundered, and the once-welcoming gates of Eden were shut behind them. They held hands as they stepped into an unknown world, their hearts heavy with loss yet ignited by the beginnings of something new—a family.

In this judgment, there is an implicit understanding of justice—God does not act out of anger but rather in response to the violation of the sacred order. The consequences serve as a reminder of the moral framework established by the Creator, reinforcing the importance of obedience and the weight of disobedience.

The Fall does not only affect Adam and Eve; it reverberates through all of creation. Their disobedience introduces sin into the world, altering the trajectory of human history. The paradise they once inhabited becomes a distant memory, replaced by a reality filled with hardship, suffering, and alienation.

The themes of shame and guilt that emerge from the Fall reflect the ongoing struggles of humanity. These feelings become intrinsic to the human experience, shaping our understanding of ourselves and our relationships with others. The loss of innocence becomes a shared narrative, resonating across generations as individuals grapple with their own moral choices and the consequences that follow.

Amidst the darkness of their disobedience, the seeds of hope are sown. The divine judgment is accompanied by a promise—a glimmer of redemption that will echo through the ages. "I will put enmity between you and the woman, and between your offspring and her offspring," God declares to the serpent, hinting at a future restoration.

This promise speaks to the enduring nature of the human spirit and the possibility of redemption, even in the face of failure. The narrative encourages readers to reflect on their own experiences of loss, choice, and the pursuit of reconciliation with the divine.

Adam and Eve's realisation of their disobedience leads to a direct confrontation with God. After Adam and Eve eat the forbidden fruit, they experience a profound transformation: they gain awareness but lose innocence. In this state of vulnerability and newfound shame, they hide, only to be sought out by God. This confrontation is filled with powerful emotions—God's sorrow over their disobedience, Adam and Eve's guilt, and the acknowledgment of the choice they made.

At this moment, God questions them, allowing each to explain. Adam, in his fear, blames Eve, while Eve attributes her choice to the serpent's deception. This cascade of blame reveals the consequences of their disobedience: it has fractured their unity and introduced division where once there was harmony. In this divine judgment, God declares consequences for each participant: the serpent is cursed to crawl and be forever alienated from humanity, Eve will bear children with pain, and Adam will toil and labour for sustenance.

These judgments reflect a transformation in their lives, symbolising humanity's new reality, where choice has weight and consequences affect more than just the self. God's judgment is not only a punishment but also an initiation into the responsibility of knowledge and the effects of choice, setting the stage for humanity's journey.

The expulsion from Eden is perhaps the most profound and sorrowful moment in the narrative. Adam and Eve are forced to leave the paradise that was their home—a place of abundance, peace, and intimacy with the divine. The imagery of Eden's gate being closed and guarded by an angel with a flaming sword highlights the finality of this separation. This act emphasises the consequences of their disobedience; they are now separated from the divine presence they once enjoyed without barrier.

The expulsion marks the beginning of a new, challenging life, one that requires effort, struggle, and resilience. The loss of Eden symbolises not only a physical change but also a spiritual one, as humanity moves from a state of unity with God to one of separation and longing. This exile represents a shift from innocence to experience, setting the stage for a life filled with questions, suffering, and the need to strive for spiritual connection and understanding.

Life outside Eden is drastically different. Adam and Eve must now contend with a world that demands labour for survival. Adam experiences the hardship of tilling soil, feeling the weight **of** physical labour that was once unnecessary in Eden. Eve, too, faces the pains of childbirth, symbolising both the continuation of life and the hardship it now entails.

Living outside Eden, Adam and Eve experience their own vulnerability and limitations, along with their capacity for growth and resilience. They come to embody the full range of human strengths and weaknesses, portraying a more complex, realistic human existence where joy and pain coexist.

Adam and Eve must adapt to their new, harsher reality. This adaptation process reflects humanity's resilience and capacity for change. Rather than living passively in paradise, they are now actively engaged in shaping their lives, learning skills, and navigating difficulties. This shift highlights human agency and the ability to find meaning, even amid loss and suffering.

Their struggle for survival represents humanity's entry into a world where sustaining life requires effort, skill, and persistence. This new life brings them into closer contact with mortality and the fragility of human existence. It is a world in which they must learn, adapt, and endure, shaping their character and deepening their understanding of both suffering and resilience. This period of struggle highlights the importance of perseverance and the strength of the human spirit when confronted with challenges. While Eden offers ease and abundance, life outside its gates becomes a journey defined by the need to overcome obstacles, shaping humanity's relationship with the natural world.

The exile from Eden carries profound symbolic weight, representing not just a physical departure but also a spiritual journey. It symbolises humanity's separation from divine intimacy and the loss of a paradise where all needs were met and all beings lived in harmony. This spiritual exile is marked by an internal yearning to restore that lost connection and regain the unity once experienced in Eden. Humanity's path is now one of spiritual growth, self-discovery, and the search for a deeper understanding of existence.

Exile is a theme echoed throughout religious and cultural traditions, where humanity's sense of displacement fuels a quest for reunion with the divine. The longing to overcome this separation motivates a journey filled with growth, wisdom, and self-reflection. This search for paradise reflects the human need for spiritual meaning and a return to a harmonious state. It is a journey filled with moral choices, lessons, and the pursuit of enlightenment, symbolising humanity's drive to overcome the barriers of exile and find purpose within the human condition.

The story of Eden has had a lasting impact on how humans perceive sin, forgiveness, and spiritual aspiration. The Eden story and exile is at the heart of mankind's quest for redemption and spiritual satisfaction in religion and philosophy. This heritage shows a general desire to reconnect with God and regain lost favour.

In Christianity, the Fall refers to the initial sin of humankind; the solution lies in redemption through faith, grace, and Christ's sacrifice. Judaism teaches that exile is overcome through repentance and returning to God—essentially seeing it as moral development and covenant renewal. Islam takes the tale as a warning about human error: Adam and Eve's actions are seen as being in a divinely preordained narrative eventually leading to mercy and forgiveness.

Beyond religious doctrines, the Eden narrative has influenced art, literature, and philosophy. It speaks to the fundamental human experience of loss, the yearning for wholeness, and the hope for a return to a state of grace. The story of Eden invites humanity to reflect on the choices that define us and our capacity for growth, forgiveness, and the pursuit of wisdom.

The legacy of Eden, then, is a reminder of both humanity's fragility and its potential for redemption—a symbol of the journey toward an understanding of self, the divine, and the quest to restore harmony in a world forever changed by the choices made in paradise.

As we conclude this chapter, we recognise the profound lessons embedded within the story of the Fall. Adam and Eve's journey from innocence to knowledge is emblematic of the human condition—marked by choices, consequences, and the quest for redemption.

The themes of disobedience and judgment invite reflection on our own moral choices and the paths we navigate in life. The Fall serves as a reminder that while humanity may stray from the divine path, the promise of redemption remains—a beacon of hope guiding us through the complexities of human existence.

INTERACTIVE ELEMENT—REFLECTIVE QUESTIONS:

When is the pursuit of knowledge empowering, and when can it be dangerous? Think of a time when curiosity led you to learn something that changed your perspective. Was it for better or for worse?

Have you ever faced a decision where you were torn between following the rules or breaking them to pursue something that felt right for you? How did you feel at that moment?

CHAPTER 5:
The Transformation—Facing a New Reality

Adam and Eve now see the world in a way they never imagined. Their choice to eat the fruit has awakened them to a new understanding, but with it comes a profound sense of vulnerability. They look at each other and realise, for the first time, their own limitations, and the complexity of their humanity. This knowledge brings them closer but also creates a distance as they struggle to deal with the awareness that they are both individuals with their own thoughts, emotions, and fears.

This awakening brings with it the weight of self-awareness. They feel exposed, recognizing the distinction between themselves and the world around them. The beauty of Eden is still present, but now they also see its fragility, its temporary nature. They feel the pull of responsibility and the understanding that every action they take has consequences.

THE BEGINNING OF SHAME AND SELF-DOUBT

One of the earliest emotions they experience is shame—an awkward, unknown emotion that separates them from a once-innocent state they didn't even realise. They begin to see their bodies differently, noticing a new nakedness in their frailty and becoming conscious of themselves as beings capable of judgment.

They cover themselves with leaves, not only to shield their bodies but as an attempt to protect their inner selves from the vulnerability they now feel. This experience of shame marks a shift in their relationship with each other and with Eden itself. No longer purely innocent beings, they are now conscious individuals who must reconcile their desires, choices, and responsibilities.

EVOLVING RELATIONSHIP DYNAMICS

Adam and Eve's newfound awareness also changes their relationship with each other. Before the Fall, their bond was simple and harmonious, grounded in mutual trust and unity. Now, with self-awareness, they experience their connection as a more complex relationship, filled with both beauty and challenge. They see each other's strengths and flaws, as well as the potential for misunderstanding and conflict.

This shift does not weaken their bond; rather, it deepens it, making it more resilient. They begin to communicate more openly, sharing their fears, hopes, and uncertainties. Adam listens to Eve's experiences, and she listens to him. They realise that they are no longer just partners in paradise, but companions on a journey that will require patience, trust, and mutual support.

They are drawn closer by this shared vulnerability, even as they learn to respect each other's individuality. Their love becomes less about harmony and more about shared understanding—a bond built on the acceptance of both light and shadow within each other.

THE BURDEN OF RESPONSIBILITY

Along with knowledge comes the weight of responsibility. Adam and Eve now understand that their choices have lasting effects on their lives and the world around them. They feel the burden of this realisation, knowing that they are no longer sheltered by the innocence of Eden. Every decision they make, every action they take, will shape their lives and the world they inhabit.

This responsibility brings a sense of purpose, but it also brings fear. They are no longer protected from hardship; they are aware of the potential for pain and loss. The garden no longer feels like a place of eternal comfort; it has become a temporary home, a place of learning and preparation for something unknown. Adam and Eve realise that they must face this reality with courage, accepting the consequences of their choices and embracing the unknown path ahead.

A NEW UNDERSTANDING OF GOOD AND EVIL

With their awareness of good and evil, Adam and Eve come to understand that the world is filled with both beauty and challenge, light and shadow. This knowledge does not make Eden less beautiful; rather, it makes it more precious, as they see its value and its impermanence. They recognise that every joy is accompanied by sorrow and that life is a balance of opposites.

Their understanding of good and evil is not simplistic; they see it as a complex interplay of forces that shape the world and their own inner lives. This duality becomes a source of wisdom, teaching them that life's true beauty lies in its complexity and depth. They realise that by embracing both the joy and the pain of existence, they are embracing the fullness of what it means to be alive.

PREPARING FOR LIFE BEYOND EDEN

Adam and Eve sense that their time in Eden is ending. They are no longer innocent beings; they are now aware, responsible, and prepared to face a new life beyond the boundaries of paradise. They feel a mixture of sadness and anticipation, knowing that their journey will be difficult but also meaningful.

Eden has been their home, their sanctuary, but they now see it as a place of growth, a foundation for the lives they are about to build. They know that leaving Eden will be painful, but they accept it as a necessary step toward becoming fully human. Together, they prepare themselves for the unknown, ready to face life's challenges with courage, love, and resilience.

A PARTNERSHIP REFORGED

Their relationship, once simple and harmonious, is now a deeper and more mature bond. They have faced the unknown together, shared in each other's vulnerabilities, and accepted the complexity of their own humanity. As they stand at the edge of Eden, Adam and Eve know that they are no longer the same. They are now partners in every sense of the word, bound not only by love but by a shared purpose and commitment to one another.

This bond will be their strength as they step into the unknown. Though Eden will always be a cherished memory, they are ready to move forward together, to embrace the world beyond its boundaries, and to create a life shaped by their own choices and experiences.

THE SYMBOLISM OF EXILE—HUMANITY'S SPIRITUAL JOURNEY

In this chapter, we also explore how the concept of exile resonates across various cultures and religions, illustrating a universal human experience. Exile is not limited to the physical displacement of Adam and Eve from the Garden of Eden; it reflects deeper spiritual and emotional truths shared by humanity throughout history.

The chapter delves deeply into the themes of exile, survival, and redemption, drawing connections between Adam and Eve's experience and the broader human journey. The expulsion from the Garden of Eden marks a pivotal moment in the narrative of Adam and Eve. This chapter explores the profound consequences of their choices, the symbolism of exile, and the enduring human struggle for survival in a world that is now fundamentally altered.

With the judgment pronounced and the consequences laid bare, Adam and Eve find themselves facing an unimaginable reality: the loss of paradise. Driven from the garden, they step into a world that is starkly different from the one they once knew. The lush greenery, the tranquil rivers, and the gentle sounds of creation are replaced by a harsh landscape filled with uncertainty and toil.

As the gates of Eden close behind them, the weight of their choices becomes palpable. The cherubim, with their flaming swords, stand guard at the entrance, symbolising the impenetrable barrier between humanity and the divine grace they once enjoyed. No longer will they walk in direct communion with God; the intimacy of their relationship has been irrevocably altered.

In Eden, Adam and Eve lived in a state of innocence, shielded from hardship and fully provided for. Outside the garden, they encounter a world where survival demands effort and where they must face the reality of death. This shift represents the human journey from innocence to experience, symbolising the growth that comes with self-awareness and responsibility.

The expulsion thrusts Adam and Eve into a new reality defined by struggle and hardship. God's judgment that Adam would toil for his sustenance takes on immediate significance. The fertile ground of Eden is replaced by soil that resists cultivation. Where once they could pluck fruit from trees with ease, now they must work tirelessly to provide for themselves.

God's pronouncement that Adam would have to work "by the sweat of his brow" to grow food symbolises humanity's struggle with nature and the environment. Adam must now labour to produce sustenance, representing a fundamental shift from abundance to scarcity. Similarly, Eve's curse of pain in childbirth points to the cost of procreation and the ongoing cycle of life.

Outside Eden, Adam and Eve are forced to develop new skills to survive, which can be seen as the beginnings of human civilisation. By cultivating the land and forming a society, they mirror humanity's movement from a foraging, idyllic existence to an agricultural, structured life. This narrative reflects the historical shift from nomadic to settled societies, with its accompanying struggles and innovations.

The stark contrast between their former life and their new existence highlights the reality of human struggle. The idyllic paradise that symbolised peace and abundance is gone, and the daily grind of survival becomes their new norm. Adam's sweat-soaked brow and Eve's aching body are tangible reminders of the consequences of their disobedience.

With the knowledge of good and evil comes the burden of moral responsibility. Adam and Eve must now navigate a world where every action has consequences. This knowledge signifies the beginning of ethical and moral awareness, representing the complex nature of human choice and accountability in the world.

Exile serves as a powerful metaphor for the human condition. It represents not only the physical separation from paradise but also the spiritual alienation from God. In this new existence, Adam and Eve experience the weight of guilt, shame, and loss—a stark reminder of the fragility of innocence.

The journey outside Eden mirrors the spiritual journeys that countless individuals face throughout history. Just as Adam and Eve grapple with their new reality, humanity grapples with the consequences of choices made in moments of temptation. Exile becomes a space for growth, reflection, and the search for meaning amidst adversity.

In the wilderness beyond Eden, Adam and Eve must learn to navigate the challenges of their new life. As they confront the realities of pain and suffering, they begin to understand the value of perseverance and resilience. Their bond as partners becomes crucial, as they lean on each other for support in their shared struggle.

Eve, experiencing the pain of childbirth, embodies the reality of human suffering. The joy of bringing new life into the world is intertwined with the agony of labour. In this way, the duality of existence is revealed, as "joy and sorrow" and "love and pain" coexist in the human experience.

Amidst the struggle, the couple also discovers the cycle of life. The harshness of their unique environment teaches them to adapt and grow. They plant seeds, nurturing them into crops, and learn the importance of community as they encounter other families facing similar challenges. The simple act of sharing becomes a source of strength, fostering connections that transcend individual hardships.

As they navigate the complexities of life outside Eden, Adam and Eve begin to redefine their understanding of purpose and fulfilment. They cultivate a relationship with the land and with one another, finding beauty in the small moments of existence. The laughter of their children, the warmth of companionship, and the beauty of a sunset become cherished aspects of their new reality.

Even in their exile, the legacy of Eden lingers in their hearts. The memory of paradise serves as a guiding light, reminding them of the divine promise and the possibility of redemption. This enduring quest for restoration becomes a central theme in human experience, echoing through generations as individuals strive to reconcile their existence with their spiritual origins.

The spiritual journey of Adam and Eve transcends their immediate circumstances; it reflects the broader narrative of humanity's quest for meaning. Across cultures and traditions, the desire for redemption resonates deeply. The longing to return to a state of grace and harmony with the divine is a thread that weaves through the human experience, shaping beliefs, art, and philosophy.

As Adam and Eve face the challenges of their new life, they cling to the promise made by God in the aftermath of their disobedience. The prophecy regarding the offspring of Eve hints at the possibility of restoration—a glimmer of hope that their journey does not end in despair.

This promise becomes a source of strength, inspiring them to persevere in their struggles. It serves as a reminder that even amidst hardship, the potential for redemption exists. Their experiences in exile become a foundation for future generations, teaching the values of humility, repentance, and the importance of seeking reconciliation with the divine.

While their relationship was altered by the Fall, Adam and Eve's journey together outside Eden also reflects the resilience and strength of partnership. They must learn to work together to survive in their new reality, suggesting the idea that relationships can evolve and strengthen through shared challenges and mutual support.

Adam and Eve's life outside Eden includes the birth of their children, Cain, Abel, and later Seth. As the first parents, they begin the lineage of humanity, representing the start of human family and community structures. This growth of family reflects the importance of connection and support in the human condition, as well as the inevitable conflicts and bonds that come with relationships.

Adam and Eve experience both the joys and sorrows of parenthood, especially with the tragic story of Cain and Abel. Cain's jealousy and his eventual murder of Abel introduce themes of sibling rivalry, moral failings, and the pain parents face when their children are in conflict. This dynamic brings to light the enduring challenges of family life, including the need for forgiveness, resilience, and hope.

In this chapter, we have explored the themes of exile, survival, and the enduring quest for redemption that arise from the expulsion from Eden. The journey of Adam and Eve serves as a poignant reminder of the complexities of the human experience—the interplay between choices, consequences, and the hope for restoration.

As they navigate their new reality, Adam and Eve embody the resilience of the human spirit. Their story invites us to reflect on our own struggles, the search for meaning, and the quest for redemption that transcends the barriers of time and space. In embracing the journey, we discover that even amid hardship, the promise of hope remains a guiding light, illuminating the path toward a deeper understanding of ourselves and our relationship with the divine.

CHAPTER 6:
Life Beyond Eden

THE QUEST FOR REDEMPTION

Weeks passed. The harsh realities beyond Eden ceased to be a transient thought; they were now an irrevocable aspect of life. Adam and Eve worked from dawn till dusk, tirelessly trying to make a living on a land that had no compassion. Still, amid crashes of hunger, against bitter cold and exhaustion, things were slowly—imperceptibly at first—changing around them, not just in the environment but within themselves.

The knowledge weighed heavily on them, albeit in unusual ways. Eve, ever the seeker, was often lost in thought as she questioned the vastness of the world and the transgressions. Knowledge had been a gift, but it had come at a cost that neither of them could fully comprehend.

Adam, meanwhile, had grown quieter. His strength was no longer only physical—though that was still an integral part of who he was—but emotional. He had taken on the responsibility of protecting Eve, of keeping them moving forward. But the weight of his role as a provider was beginning to erode the confidence he had once felt.

One afternoon, as the sun cast shadows across the jagged horizon, Eve sat by a fire and absentmindedly picked at rough edges of a rock she had found earlier in the day. Adam sat beside her, carving tools in hand, but his mind was elsewhere. He had always been a person of action, someone who worked hard and found his sense of purpose in creating, building, and protecting. But now, as they tried to eke out a living in a world that seemed determined to test their limits, he found himself questioning everything.

"Do you ever wonder," Eve said suddenly, breaking the silence, "if we made the right choice?"

Adam did not look up immediately, his hands automatically shaping the wood before him. The question hung in the air between them, heavy with its implications.

He replied softly, "We didn't have a choice, Eve. We couldn't stay ignorant forever."

Eve's brow furrowed. She was not sure if it was a question she was asking him, or one she was asking herself. They had both been given the same command, and they had both disobeyed it, choosing to taste the forbidden fruit. And yet, the burden of that choice felt different in their hearts.

"Sometimes," Eve continued, eyeing the distance with a far-off look in her eyes "I feel like we were meant for something more. That we were always meant to be more than just caretakers of Eden."

Adam glanced at her then, seeing the faraway look in her eyes. The ambition and curiosity that had led her to the tree were still there, undimmed; if anything, they had only grown.

"What if it was too much?" Adam asked softly, weariness creeping into his voice. "What if we couldn't handle it?"

Eve did not answer immediately. Instead, she stood and walked to the edge of their camp, staring out into the darkening landscape. She said, "Maybe we're supposed to bear it all—the weight of our actions and the knowledge we've gained. Maybe it wasn't about what we were meant to be, but rather the choice of who we become now."

Adam stood and joined her, his gaze following hers across the barren land. The world outside Eden might be cruel, but it was also brimming with potential. They had been given the gift of knowledge, but that did not mean they were condemned to failure. Perhaps, in the face of this harsh new reality, they could find redemption.

"We'll have to work harder than we ever have before," Adam said, his voice firm but gentle. "But we're not alone in this; We are together."

Eve looked up at him, a slow smile beginning to form on her lips. "Together. Yes. We are."

"Eve, even now, even here…our love is not lost. It flickers, yes, but it will not die." He took her hand in his, his voice low and steady:

> The look of you gives me pleasure.
> The joy you give is a treasure.
> The life we live is not easy.
> The life we face will be busy.
> I know the wind will always blow,
> And the river will dance and flow.
> I know I will always love you,
> Whether far or near, in all I do.

And in that moment, amidst the vast expanse of a world they had only just begun to understand, they found something they had not expected: Hope. It was fragile, delicate, like the first buds of spring breaking through frozen soil. But it was there, rooted in the bond they shared.

The story of Adam and Eve in the Garden of Eden is not merely a tale of innocence lost; it is also a narrative deeply rooted in the quest for redemption. Across cultures and religious traditions, the themes of Fall and Restoration resonate, offering insights into the human condition. This chapter will explore the nature of redemption as understood in various faiths, delve into philosophical reflections on growth, discuss lessons relevant to today's world, and reflect on Eden's legacy in our lives.

In the garden, Adam and Eve were close to God. Outside of it, they experienced a new way of interacting with the divine—one that was less immediate and more distanced. God is no longer as present or approachable, symbolising the human journey to seek meaning, faith, and connection in a world where divine guidance is less immediate. This change reflects the human quest for spirituality and understanding in the face of life's hardships.

Leaving Eden is both a physical and emotional journey for Adam and Eve. They cross the boundary that once protected them, stepping into a landscape vastly different from the paradise they knew. The world outside Eden was beautiful, but untamed; rugged terrain lay, vast skies stretched, and the unknown loomed. For the first time, they face the rawness of nature and the reality of survival.

They feel a mixture of sadness and excitement. The comfort of Eden is behind them, but a world of potential awaits. As they walk together, they realise that every step they take is a step into the unknown. This realisation strengthens their bond as they cling to each other for support, each aware that they are the only two humans in this vast, new world.

Leaving Eden comes to symbolise estrangement from God and the need for redemption. This longing for a return to unity with the divine represents the human spiritual journey—one that involves searching for meaning, moral guidance, and forgiveness or reconciliation.

Life outside Eden requires adaptation. In Eden, food was abundant, the weather was mild, and all of creation lived in harmony. Now, Adam and Eve must learn the rhythms of nature, understanding that life is no longer predictable or easily provided. They learn to gather food, recognise plants and animals, and develop the skills needed to survive.

This adaptation is challenging but empowering. For the first time, they feel the satisfaction of their own labour. Each task, from gathering fruit to building shelter, brings a sense of accomplishment and pride.

They learn to appreciate the natural world in a new way, seeing its beauty alongside its hardships. They come to understand that survival is a partnership with the earth, and they find a sense of purpose in working together to build a life from what the land provides.

Their new life also brings hardship, something they had never known in Eden. They feel hunger, fatigue, and the weight of physical labour. They experience discomfort as they adjust to the seasons, the harshness of the elements, and the dangers of the natural world. They learn that life is fragile, that they are vulnerable, and that survival requires resilience and determination.

Through these hardships, they come to realise the value of each moment. The fleeting nature of comfort and peace makes them cherish each joyful experience, no matter how small. They also grow stronger, both physically and emotionally, as they face challenges together. Hardship becomes a teacher, imparting lessons on endurance, resilience, and the strength that comes from enduring difficulties.

Loss becomes a new and painful part of their existence. They see creatures around them experience sickness, injury, and death, and they understand that they, too, are mortal. This awareness deepens their appreciation for life, teaching them the importance of cherishing each day. The loss of Eden becomes more poignant, but they also find a new appreciation for the life they are building with each other, filled with moments of both struggle and joy.

THE EVOLUTION OF THEIR RELATIONSHIP

The challenges they face transform their relationship in profound ways. Once companions living peacefully in Eden, they are now united as partners in survival. They start to rely on each other like never before, helping while bonding in trying situations. Their relationship grows stronger with each challenge they face, witnessing every bit of the other's firmness, patience, and kindness.

Adam takes on a protective role, working to provide shelter and safety, while Eve finds new ways to nurture and support their lives. They find equilibrium in roles and responsibilities, respecting each other's strengths and weaknesses. Now their partnership is based on something more than companionship—it has a shared purpose and faithfulness imbued with the understanding they are the only two allies in this new world.

Working side by side, they discover new dimensions in each other. They discover a new depth of courage, determination, and capacity for love in each other when confronted with hardship.

Love matures as it experiences the trials of life, from Eden's innocence to a resilient and enduring love. This love becomes their greatest strength, carrying them through the uncertainties and difficulties of life beyond paradise.

DISCOVERING COMMUNITY AND LEGACY

Adam and Eve eventually see their journey as more than survival; it is about leaving a legacy. There is hope for the future—and meaning to their lives—as they dream that their struggle and sacrifices would lay a foundation for others who follow. As they watch other creatures reproduce and multiply, the thought of children or a family brings new hope and purpose to their lives, a vision of a community that will grow from their labour and love.

They begin to prepare for this future, building a home, establishing routines, and setting down roots. Every step is intentional, knowing they're laying a foundation for family who'll carry on after them. They envision a world where their descendants thrive, learning from the lessons they have and passing them on—creating lives of significance.

Family brings joy and duty. Knowing this kept them living purposefully to create a life in accordance with the values they have found—resilience, compassion, and strength of human connection.

EMBRACING THEIR HUMANITY

Their journey from Eden to this new life is ultimately a journey of becoming fully human. They have embraced the complexities of existence, facing both joy and sorrow, comfort, and hardship. Having gone through experiences, they realised that life is beautiful in its challenges—and love weaves meaning into each moment.

Adam and Eve accept that they are no longer innocent beings, but they find peace in their new understanding. They are not perfect, but they are whole. They have gained knowledge, faced hardship, and discovered their own strength. By embracing both light and shadow within themselves, they have embraced the fullness of their humanity.

As they look over the land that has become their home, they feel deeply fulfilled. They are no longer Adam and Eve of Eden; they are individuals who have grown, struggled, and come together in love and resilience. They found a new paradise within each other—not one of innocence, but one of acceptance, understanding, and enduring love.

SEEDS OF KNOWLEDGE: THE ENDURING TALE OF THE GARDEN OF EDEN

Before the temptation in Eden, Adam and Eve lived in a state of innocence, perceiving only the goodness of their surroundings. They resided in a harmonious world, where the idea of "evil" or moral wrongness was unknown to them.

Their view of Eden was pure and untainted by the intricacies and duality of human experience. However, by eating from the Tree of Knowledge of Good and Evil, they realised an awareness that changed their lives fundamentally: From knowledge of good alone to knowledge of good *and* evil!

1.   **The Awakening to Moral Duality**

In the beginning, Adam and Eve did not differentiate between good and evil; they merely lived in a state of innocent trust and natural harmony with their environment. Without the knowledge of good and evil, they did not perceive anything as forbidden or dangerous. Their world was entirely "good" because they did not have a concept of its opposite.

After the serpent succeeded in convincing Adam and Eve to eat the fruit, they obtained this duality of knowledge that brought them into a state of moral consciousness. This knowledge allowed them to understand the concept of "wrong" for the first time, making them aware of the potential for harm, suffering, and moral choice. This duality changed their perception of the world, as they could now see both the good and the flaws in themselves.

2.   **The Experience of Shame and Self-Awareness**

One of the first effects of the knowledge of good and evil was a new awareness of their nakedness. Before this, they had been unashamed in their natural state; however, with the knowledge, they felt exposed and vulnerable. This exposure led to the awareness of shame, and to an emotional response to their understanding of themselves as separate, morally aware beings capable of judgment.

Their innocence was replaced by self-consciousness, a realisation that made them view themselves and each other in a new, critical light. They became aware of themselves as individuals with distinct, autonomous wills, leading to a sense of separateness that disrupted their prior unity and harmony.

3.   **Fear and Alienation**

After their disobedience, Adam and Eve felt fear for the first time. Hearing God approach, they hid out of fear—knowing He had given a command that they had broken. This fear was a direct result of their awareness of wrongdoing, reflecting the inner conflict that arises from the knowledge of evil.

Their awareness of good and evil created a sense of alienation, not only from God but also from each other. Where there was once innocence and trust, there was now guilt and mistrust. They no longer felt at ease in each other's presence, signifying the impact that moral awareness and shame had on their relationship.

4.   The Burden of Moral Responsibility

With the knowledge of good and evil came a newfound responsibility. Adam and Eve now understood that their actions had consequences, and they had to face those consequences. This awareness was the beginning of human moral agency—it marks humanity's ability to choose, often between right and wrong, and thus bear the weight of their choices.

The moral complexity introduced by this knowledge meant that life could no longer be simple and straightforward. They had to navigate a world where their actions carried moral significance, introducing the potential for regret, doubt, and ethical dilemmas. Their newfound understanding marked the end of the carefree existence they had enjoyed in Eden.

5.   Recognition of Suffering and Mortality

Part of the knowledge of good and evil includes the understanding of suffering. God declared that Adam and Eve in their toil and labour would experience pain, reflecting a new awareness of life's hardships. This awareness was a profound shift from their previous existence, where they had known only ease and abundance.

The awareness of evil also brought with it the concept of death, a concept they had previously been shielded from in Eden. This realisation introduced a new, existential dimension to their lives, one marked by the understanding of their own limitations and the inevitable end of life. Their new perspective on mortality created a sense of urgency and fragility that would forever shape their existence outside Eden.

6.   Impact on Their Perception of Nature and the World

Before their disobedience, Adam and Eve viewed Eden as a place of perfect beauty and harmony. However, with the knowledge of evil, they could no longer perceive the world as wholly good. They became aware of the potential for suffering, struggle, and harm within the world itself. Nature, once their harmonious home, became a place of toil and survival.

Adam and Eve's relationship with the natural world grew more complex. Where there was once peaceful coexistence, now there was labour and struggle. They could no longer take the abundance of Eden for granted, and their new awareness changed how they related to the land, animals, and to each other.

7.   Emergence of Conflict and Ethical Decision-Making

The knowledge of good and evil sets the stage for the first human conflicts, as exemplified in the story of Cain and Abel. The awareness of moral difference, choice, and consequence paved the way for jealousy, resentment, and ethical struggles that had not existed in Eden. This change in human relations brought new challenges to their lives.

Adam and Eve's awareness of good and evil set the stage for moral and ethical decision-making, a fundamental aspect of human life. They must now operate in a world outside Eden, where choosing between right and wrong became an ongoing aspect of their lives, creating responsibility that reflected on moral growth. This framework shaped not only their individual lives but the lives of all future generations, emphasising the importance of moral discernment in human society.

8.   The Quest for Redemption and Meaning

The knowledge of evil introduced a sense of loss and separation from God, and with it a yearning to restore the lost unity they had once experienced. This desire is a foundational theme in many religious traditions, symbolising humanity's search for reconciliation and redemption. Their story, thus, becomes one of seeking meaning and understanding in a morally complex world.

In their innocence, Adam and Eve experienced life as entirely sacred. After acquiring knowledge, they became aware of the profane, realising that the world contains both divine and mundane elements. This duality adds depth to human spirituality, encouraging a search for the sacred within a world that also holds imperfection and evil.

IN SUMMARY

The knowledge of evil completely changed Adam and Eve's lives with moral complexity, self-awareness, and an understanding about hardship and mortality. Their new view of the world evolved from an innocent perception of pure goodness (in Eden) to one that includes suffering, choice, and consequence.

This knowledge marks the beginning of human consciousness and moral responsibility, setting them on a journey that involves ethical decision-making, resilience, and the quest for meaning. Instead of seeing Eden as a state they could return to, they now must navigate life with the awareness of good and evil, bearing the weight of their choices and striving for purpose in a morally intricate world.

CHAPTER 7:

Seeds of the Future: The Beginning
of Family and Legacy

THE LONGING FOR FAMILY

Outside Eden, Adam and Eve grow closer in their relationship, resulting in a longing to build a family. This desire to nurture life marks their evolution from being caretakers of Eden to becoming creators of a new world in which they can pass down learned values and wisdom. Their vision of family is shared, and it gives them joy and hope—a chance to create a future that will reflect their journey, on which they have grown.

The thought of having children adds a new dimension to their lives—it motivates them in their labour and connects them as well. They envision a community that extends beyond themselves, a lineage carrying forth the lessons of resilience, compassion, and the emotional connection they have learned.

THE GIFT AND CHALLENGE OF PARENTHOOD

When Adam and Eve have their first child, they feel amazed and thankful. They see their child as both a new life and a continuation of themselves. However, parenting comes with challenges: They must figure out how to provide care, nurturing, instruction, and guidance without Eden's protections in place. Their duty now extends to founding their family and creating a legacy.

In parenthood, they discover a deeper understanding of both love and sacrifice. Each day comes with new demands and joys as they navigate the balance between their own needs and those of their children. Parenthood requires patience, resilience, and accepting life's unpredictability. Through their children, they feel the vulnerability of love—knowing that another's well-being is now tied to their own.

PASSING DOWN LESSONS OF RESILIENCE AND COMPASSION

As their family grows, Adam and Eve share stories of Eden with their children, imparting both the beauty and challenges of their journey. They talk about choosing knowledge and awareness over innocence, not just paradise. They encourage their children to be curious, self-aware, and brave in facing life's uncertainties.

These stories help their children understand that life's beauty lies in both its joys and its challenges. Adam and Eve explain to them the significance of resilience, demonstrating that hardship is not a punishment but rather a teacher—an opportunity to unearth strength and wisdom. Through their struggles, they learned lessons of compassion and kindness—traits that are essential for their children to carry into their own journeys.

Their children come to see their parents as more than figures of authority; they are role models, people who have lived fully, faced hardship, and emerged with grace and gratitude. Adam and Eve's legacy becomes a blend of strength and empathy, a foundation for the family that will carry their values into the future.

BUILDING A COMMUNITY

As time passes and their children grow, Adam and Eve's family begins to resemble a small community. Everyone pitches in, and all roles are seen as valuable and necessary. Adam and Eve watch with pride as their children learn to cooperate, to respect one another, and to celebrate each other's strengths. This community stands as proof of the shared efforts they have put in, and as living embodiments of values instilled by them.

Their family becomes more than a source of comfort; it is a partnership rooted in shared purpose. Together, they learn the importance of teamwork, respect, and the balance between individual freedom and collective responsibility. Adam and Eve see in their family the beginnings of a society; a community based on mutual support, where each member is valued and where love and resilience are central to their way of life.

THE CYCLE OF LEGACY

As they age, Adam and Eve witness the results of their efforts in their children and community. They watch as their children pass down the values they have learned, continuing the legacy of resilience, compassion, and gratitude. Their descendants learn from Eden's stories and Adam and Eve's wisdom, becoming caretakers and creators. This cycle of legacy brings a sense of peace and fulfilment to Adam and Eve. They understand that their lives were not just about surviving beyond Eden but also of laying the groundwork for future generations. Their legacy is not simply a memory of paradise but a lasting influence on the lives of those who follow—a heritage built on love, growth, and the courage to embrace the fullness of human experience.

A FINAL REFLECTION

When Adam and Eve reflect on their journey, they realise that it was not the Fall from Eden that defined their lives but rather what choices they made after the Fall. They chose to seek understanding, to embrace the unknown, and to build a life founded on love and resilience. This journey, marked by both joy and hardship, has become a story of transformation and renewal.

In their family and community, they see the continuation of this journey—a new generation that will carry forward the lessons of their lives. Adam and Eve feel a deep sense of peace, knowing that they have lived fully, loved deeply, and left a legacy that will endure.

Their story is no longer one of lost innocence but of a life embraced in all its complexity, a life defined by the strength of love and the courage to face the unknown. As they look upon their family, they know that their journey was not in vain. They have become creators of a new world, a world built not on innocence, but on the strength of human connection and the enduring power of love.

CHAPTER 8

The Physical Transformation of Adam and Eve

The relationship between Adam and Eve is essential to the biblical themes of companionship, family, and the propagation of humankind. Once they were driven out from Eden, Adam and Eve entered a new phase of life that involved physical intimacy that led to conception and childbirth—beginning with Cain.

In Genesis, the story of Adam and Eve indicates a moment in their relationship when they discover, transform, and begin life outside of Eden. This journey encompasses their growing physical and emotional connection, the emergence of sexuality, and the experience of pregnancy and childbirth—now marked by physical pain as God had forewarned would be the consequence of Eve's choice.

DISCOVERING PHYSICAL INTIMACY: A NATURAL EXPRESSION OF CONNECTION

In the Garden of Eden, Adam and Eve are portrayed as being in a state of innocence and unity. Sexuality between them is introduced gradually as they learn about their bodies, emotions, and desires in a new context, especially after attaining the knowledge of good and evil.

Their physical intimacy probably started as an instinctual act, a natural consequence of closeness that drew them together and reinforced their bond—mirroring the unity they shared in Eden albeit without the innocence of their prior state.

After the Fall, Adam and Eve became aware that physical intimacy was not only a means of unity but also an expression of love, comfort, and common purpose. This intimacy acquired more layers of meaning, as it was no longer merely a part of their uncorrupted state in Eden but also provided connection for them through the struggles of their new life. The development and commencement of their physical intimacy will be fully explained in a sequel to this book.

A NEW CHAPTER BEGINS

As Adam and Eve ventured further into the world, their lives that were once centered on a struggle to survive and rebuild after the Fall now became full of new experiences, perspectives, and challenges.

Eve, having embraced the unknown and the new opportunities it presented, also found herself yearning for something deeper. She now realised that rediscovering the world was only part of her journey; healing those wounds from the past also played a role. It was not just a physical journey—they had embarked on a spiritual and emotional one as well.

It was during this emotionally transformative time that Eve realised she was pregnant. The news was both a surprise and a deep, profound blessing. This pregnancy filled Eve with quiet hope. She knew that this child would be a part of their continued journey in the world, a symbol of their healing, and a testament to the resilience of life.

The full story of this pregnancy shall be explained in the sequel to this book, which will discuss the births of Cain, Abel, Seth, and their female siblings, and how these siblings also became physically intimate to create their own families over time.

For Adam, the pregnancy was a cause for joy and uncertainty. Would he be able to be the father his child needed? Would the lessons they had learned in their Fall and through their years of wandering be enough to guide their child?

It was with this deep reflection that Adam began to feel the weight of fatherhood in a way he hadn't anticipated. He wasn't just bringing a child into the world—he was shaping the future of humanity, one small life at a time.

THE BIRTH OF CAIN

Parenting is challenging under the best of circumstances. For Adam and Eve, the task was monumental. Cast out of Eden, they had no guidance, no precedent, and limited knowledge. This section explores their difficulties as the first parents in human history and how their parenting struggles, which shaped humanity's first family, set a precedent for generations. Their story reflects universal themes of love, struggle, and the hope that children will build a better future.

After a prolonged period of waiting, a son was born to them. Cain's birth was a moment of profound significance for Adam and Eve. After the Fall from Eden, their lives had been marked by grief and loss (starting with the death of Abel), and a yearning for something to heal the rift between them and the world.

The birth of their first child, a son, was a tangible sign that despite the trials they faced, life could begin anew. They named him Cain, a name meaning "acquired" or "gift," signifying the hope they had placed in him as their firstborn.

Cain was a bright child, full of energy and curiosity. From the moment he could crawl, he explored his surroundings, always eager to understand the world. Adam and Eve were amazed by his quickness to learn, his deep curiosity, and his intense need to understand the world around him. They created a new Eden for him—an Eden forged by themselves, bound not in perfection but in love and lessons of hardship.

For Eve, the act of bearing Cain felt like a form of redemption. To her, he was a chance at restarting and rebuilding what had been lost in Eden. It was a bittersweet joy. While the happiness of motherhood was undeniable, Eve carried a deep awareness of the mistakes that had led to their expulsion from paradise. Cain's birth represented not only a new life but also a reconciliation with the future.

As she held her newborn child in her hands, Eve traced the curve of Cain's tiny fingers, marvelling at the warmth of new life. The pain of birth had faded, replaced by a swelling joy she had never known. She held him close, pressing her lips to his forehead, whispering words born from the depths of her heart:

With trembling hands, I hold you near,
A gift of love, so pure, so dear.
My heart is full, my soul takes flight,
For dawn has broken from the night.

Through weary toil, through aching cries,
A child is born before my eyes.
From dust we came, yet now I see

A new life through Adam and me.

O Cain, my son, my greatest prize,
I see the world within your eyes.
No Eden's walls, no garden bright,
Yet love still shines, a guiding light.

Though sorrow shaped the path we tread,
Hope is born where fears once led.
For in your breath, so soft and true,
A mother's love is made anew.

Tears welled in her eyes, but they were no longer tears of sorrow. The weight of exile, of toil and struggle, seemed lighter now. In Cain's breath, in the way he nestled against her, she found purpose; she found love reborn.

While the happiness of motherhood was undeniable, Eve carried a deep awareness of the mistakes that had led to their expulsion from paradise. Cain's birth represented not only a new life but also a reconciliation with the future.

Adam, too, felt a surge of love and protectiveness for his newborn son. In Cain, he saw the continuation of his own lineage—a chance to impart that which had been learned through his efforts to struggle and survive. Yet there was also a weight of responsibility that Adam could not ignore.

He knew that Cain would grow up in a world far different from the one he had imagined during his days in Eden. The birth of Cain marked the beginning of a new chapter, not only in their lives, but also in the evolution of humankind.

Adam knelt beside Eve, his eyes fixed on the child in her arms. Cain stirred, stretching tiny limbs, his first breath filling the space between them. Adam's heart ached—not with sorrow, but with something new, something he had longed for since the day they left Eden. He lifted his eyes to the heavens, whispering:

O son of mine, my greatest prize,
I see the world within your eyes.
From dust we rose, from earth we came,
Yet life now speaks your sacred name.

Through weary days and endless strife,
You are the proof of love and life.
No Eden's streams, no Garden's grace,
Yet joy still shines upon your face.

O Cain, my child, my flesh, my bone,
Through you, our love is fully known.
A father's heart, so fierce, so true,
Now beats with hope because of you.

Through toil and sweat, through trials deep,
For you, my hands will plant and reap.
And though the road ahead is wide,
My love will be there by your side.

His fingers brushed over Cain's soft skin, awe settling deep in his soul. He had lost much, but at this moment, he had gained more than he could have imagined.

In those early moments, both Adam and Eve felt an overwhelming sense of purpose: to raise this child with love, wisdom, and care. They had experienced the Fall and understood the gravity of their choices, and they were determined to guide their son in a way that would help him avoid the same pitfalls. Their focus was on providing Cain with the emotional and spiritual foundation to navigate the complexities of a post-Eden world.

GOD'S PRONOUNCEMENT ON CHILDBIRTH PAIN: A MANIFESTATION OF PHYSICAL AND EMOTIONAL LABOUR

After the Fall, God declares that Eve's experience of childbirth will be marked by pain: "I will greatly increase your pains in childbearing; with pain you will give birth to children" (Genesis 3:16). This pronouncement suggests that what would have been a natural and effortless part of their life in Eden, is now altered.

Childbirth becomes a process fraught with labour, discomfort, and sometimes fear—a reminder of the consequences of their choice to seek knowledge and independence. The manifestation of this pain may be both physical and emotional. The physical pain of childbirth signifies the harsh reality of survival outside Eden, marking their transition from an existence of ease to one that demands sacrifice.

Emotionally, Eve's experience may be layered with uncertainty, anxiety, and even guilt, as she faces the reality of bringing a child into a world of toil and struggle. This profound experience reinforces Eve's understanding of life's fragility and the cost of knowledge, teaching her resilience, strength, and the significance of nurturing a new life.

CHILDBIRTH AS AN ACT OF LOVE AND SACRIFICE

Eve's experience of childbirth also represents an act of sacrifice, underscoring the depth of her love for her child. The physical pain she endures is part of her journey toward embracing motherhood, a role that requires resilience and devotion. The broader theme about human life after Eden finds its echo in this transformation—love is ever accompanied by sacrifice and hardship but becomes more meaningful as a result.

For Adam, seeing Eve in pain adds an emotional burden likely filled with responsibility and empathy. Sharing this experience allows them to understand the reality of parenthood; it also brings them closer to each other. This process strengthens their relationship, teaching them both patience, endurance, and purpose as they prepare to raise their children in a world that still holds spaces for love and connection.

THE RIPPLE EFFECT: EMOTIONAL AND SPIRITUAL SIGNIFICANCE OF CHILDBEARING

Eve's experience of childbirth, with all its pain and joy, adds a spiritual layer to her understanding of life. The act of bringing life into the world humbles her and teaches reverence, mirroring how she is related to Creation. This experience also reaffirms her relationship with God, as she recognizes the beauty and sacredness of life despite the pain involved.

Each new child born to Adam and Eve represents hope and continuity. While childbirth may serve as a reminder of their exile from Eden, it comes to symbolize renewal; and building a new life through love and resilience has its own beauty.

UNDERSTANDING SEXUALITY AND PARENTHOOD AS SACRED RESPONSIBILITIES

Adam and Eve's understanding of sexuality becomes deeply intertwined with the responsibility of parenthood. Sexuality now, unlike in Eden where they lived carefreely, is imbued with purpose and consequence, shaping them as partners and parents. Their relationship becomes sacred as they realise intimacy to be not only a means of creating life but also a shared legacy.

This understanding of sex and parenthood as sacred responsibilities becomes central to their identity and values. Their experience fosters a sense of gratitude, as each new child represents an opportunity to build a world of love, resilience, and meaning, even in the face of hardship. This cycle of creation, birth, and nurturing, while accompanied by pain, ultimately affirms their role in God's creation and deepens their commitment to one another.

A PROFOUND TRANSFORMATION: LOVE BEYOND INNOCENCE

Discovering sex and experiencing childbirth marks Adam and Eve's transformation from innocence to experience. Their love, now extending beyond Eden's simplicity, embraces the sacrifices, endurance, and resilience that come with life outside paradise. Through this journey, they find a new kind of beauty—one rooted in love tested by hardship and made more meaningful through their shared struggles.

This transformation is a powerful lesson in human experience, as Adam and Eve embrace the reality of life after Eden. Their relationship deepens as they grow into their roles as parents, sharing both joy and sorrow as they face the challenges of parenthood together. By doing so, they exemplify a love that persists beyond innocence, one which is strengthened and rendered more meaningful by the resilience they discover in each other through sharing of new life.

A NEW UNDERSTANDING OF LIFE AND LOVE

The story of Adam and Eve's discovery of intimacy and the pain of childbirth reflects a journey of transformation, responsibility, and spiritual growth. By creating life together, they share in the joys and challenges of parenthood, and embracing a love strengthened by hardship and enriched by resilience. Their story reminds us that beauty can arise from struggle and profound connection through love, even in a world changed forever.

THE GENESIS OF HUMAN COMPANIONSHIP AND UNION

From the outset, Adam and Eve's relationship is described as unique and intimate. Genesis relates that God made Eve from Adam's rib to be his "helper" and partner, indicating they are meant to complement each other. The phrase "bone of my bones and flesh of my flesh" emphasises a deep bond between them, both physically and emotionally. This partnership reflects a unity that goes beyond mere companionship; it implies a sharing of life, purpose, and experiences in their relationship.

After their expulsion from Eden, Adam and Eve are united not only in purpose but in navigating the hardships of the world together. Through shared experiences of loss and responsibility, their relationship becomes a model for family and partnership.

SEXUAL UNION AS AN EXPRESSION OF BONDING AND CONTINUATION OF LIFE

The sexual union between Adam and Eve, implied after they exited Eden, serves as a means of intimacy and procreation. Genesis 4:1 state: "Adam knew Eve, his wife; and she conceived and bore Cain." The term "knew" (Hebrew: "yada") is noteworthy because it connotes a physical and deeper, personal intimacy. The language suggests that their sexual union was not just about making babies but also an expression of love and intimacy connecting them on various levels.

This union signifies the dawn of life outside the Garden of Eden, where they take on roles not just as husband and wife but now also as father and mother. In this new life beyond paradise, sex becomes a natural mode for them to fulfil God's mandate to "be fruitful and multiply," bearing the first human family.

EVE'S PREGNANCY AND THE PAIN OF CHILDBIRTH

Eve's pregnancy with Cain symbolises both aspiration and adversity. After the Fall, God told Eve that her pains in childbearing would be multiplied—a direct result of the knowledge she obtained from eating the forbidden fruit. Her pregnancy and the eventual birth of Cain signify the mixed blessings of life outside Eden. She brings life into this world with the knowledge she gained by watching the animals go through pregnancy and birth. But with that knowledge comes pain and challenges—the inevitable human experience.

Despite these challenges, her pregnancy is a fundamental milestone in human history, as she becomes the mother of the firstborn human, Cain. This process of pregnancy and birth reveals the profound way Adam and

Eve's relationship transitions into the roles of parents, with new responsibilities and bonds that deepen their relationship.

THE BIRTH OF CAIN AND THE BEGINNING OF THE HUMAN FAMILY

When Cain was born, Adam and Eve faced all the joys and difficulties of parenthood. Cain represents the first generation after Adam and Eve, establishing the family structure that will continue through their descendants. Cain's birth signifies the beginning of a lineage that will expand into humanity; and Eve's words, "I have gotten a man with the help of the Lord," reflect both gratitude and perhaps the acknowledgment of the divine role in creating life.

CAIN'S ROLE IN THE NARRATIVE OF HUMAN PROGRESSION AND MORALITY

Cain's life and actions eventually lead to some of the Bible's earliest discussions on morality, responsibility, and human relationships. Though Adam and Eve provided the foundation for family dynamics, Cain's story explores sibling relationships, personal choice, and the consequences of human actions. When Cain enters rivalry with his brother Abel and eventually commits fratricide, tragedy comes into the family—showing how the consequences of the Fall extend into human relationships and morality.

CAIN'S LATER CHILDHOOD: A RESTLESS SPIRIT

As Cain grew, it became clear that he was a child of both deep curiosity and intense restlessness. From an early age, he exhibited an insatiable need to explore and understand the world around him. He would plunge headfirst into endless questions—from asking about the earth itself to inquiring after the mysteries of the stars above. His mind was constantly churning, trying to piece together the bigger picture of the world.

But as he entered later childhood, certain tensions began to arise within Cain. While he loved his parents and admired their strength, he found himself increasingly dissatisfied with the world they had created. Adam and

Eve had accepted the loss of Eden, but Cain felt a longing inside him—a desire to reconnect with something nameless. He felt disconnected from the world they lived in. Something was missing, and he was not sure what it was.

Cain's restlessness was compounded by the feeling that he was expected to follow in his parents' footsteps. Adam, though loving, often pushed him to embrace the lessons of survival and the wisdom of the earth. With her nurturing nature, Eve encouraged Cain to appreciate beauty, creation, and the world around him. Yet neither of them seemed to understand the deeper questions Cain had.

While Cain was taught to value the fruits of the land, the animals, and the stability that came from farming, he was drawn to more abstract thoughts—questions of existence, the nature of good and evil, and the meaning behind their lives. These musings left him isolated: He could not always explain what was bothering him, but there was a growing sense that the answers his parents gave were not enough for his restless heart.

He would often wander alone into the fields, away from the safety of their home, to find some form of solace. It was during these moments of solitude that Cain's thoughts began to mature into more complex ideas. He began to sense that he was on the edge of something bigger, something outside the world his parents had crafted. There was a deep yearning for more inside of him—a force that would eventually set him on the path of rebellion and discovery.

CAIN'S RELATIONSHIP WITH HIS PARENTS: THE STRUGGLES OF LOVE AND INDEPENDENCE

The relationship between Cain and his parents was complex and evolving. Adam and Eve were deeply invested in raising Cain to be a strong, thoughtful individual. But their differing approaches created moments of tension.

Adam, shaped by his experiences in Eden, had become protective and cautious. He emphasised the importance of hard work, the security of their land, and the need to live by the lessons they had learned from the Fall. While he interpreted Cain's inquisitive disposition as strength, he also feared that Cain's inherent restlessness might lead him down dangerous paths; the same paths Adam had once walked in the Garden.

In contrast, Eve was more in tune with Cain's feelings. She recognised his adventurous spirit, creativity, and potential within him. She encouraged him to see the world as more than just labour, but a place alive with possibility.

Though that connection enabled her to better resonate with Cain's internal struggles, Eve too was wrestling with doubt. For example, she wondered if she had the right to guide Cain in a way that might liberate him from making the very same mistakes she had made in Eden.

Cain found his parents' influence on him slightly suffocating at times. He could see the care in their actions, but he did not always understand their motivations. He started to rebel quietly rather than outright.

His desire for independence grew stronger, and with it came the feeling that he was being held back from something important. He resented the control his parents seemed to have over his life, even though they only wanted what was best for him. Cain's need to break free from their influence became a crucial point of conflict within their relationship.

CAIN'S NEED FOR INDEPENDENCE: THE SEED OF REBELLION

As Cain grew older, his rebelliousness increased. He became more frustrated with his parents' guidance. He wanted to explore the world on his own terms and make his own choices; but there was always a sense of guilt that came with stepping away from the values his parents had instilled in him. He knew they loved him; but the more he grew, the more Cain realized that his life was not meant to mirror theirs. He could not just follow their path; he had to create his own.

These early years were the seeds planted to influence Cain's eventual departure. His growing independence led to conflicts with Adam, who was trying to instil discipline and responsibility in him; and Eve, who sought to protect him from making the same mistakes she'd made. Cain's struggle was not only against authority, but also a deep yearning for something more than the familiar world his parents had known.

PARENTING AND THE STRUGGLE FOR BALANCE

Adam and Eve's contrasting approaches to raising Cain highlight the delicate balance between protection and freedom. While Adam is cautious and protective, Eve is more nurturing, encouraging Cain's independence. This tension shapes Cain's development and foreshadows his eventual rebellion.

THE QUEST FOR IDENTITY

Cain's struggles to define himself apart from his parents mirror the universal journey of adolescence and early adulthood. As Cain seeks to understand his place in the world, he experiences the growing pains of self-discovery and the frustration of trying to balance familial expectations with personal desires.

INDEPENDENCE VS. CONNECTION

The chapter also explores Cain's need for independence, which grows alongside his desire to connect with something deeper than the world his parents have known. His journey reflects the tension between the desire to break free and the need for connection to, and understanding from, his family.

THE EVOLUTION OF ADAM AND EVE'S RELATIONSHIP; AND HUMANITY'S BEGINNINGS

Adam and Eve's relationship, which starts innocently in harmony, passes through companionship, marriage, and parenthood. Their relationship evolves with the new world outside Eden; and they eventually have children, whose presence further deepens matters by expanding human love, sexuality, and family into the biblical narrative. The birth of Cain thus signifies not only the emergence of a human family, but also an onset of struggles typical to humans regarding morality and relationships coupled with responsibility.

Thus, Adam and Eve's relationship has been seen as a pivotal part of the biblical narrative by illustrating love, growth, and family themes about human history.

One evening as the sun began to set, its golden light illuminating everything around them, Eve noticed something. A small figure was walking toward them, stumbling slightly as it approached. Her heart skipped a beat.

"Adam," she trembled in a whisper. "Do you see that?"

Adam turned, following her gaze. "Is that a child?" he softly asked with disbelief.

A boy, no older than a few years, stood before them, his eyes wide with wonder. His skin was a shade darker than theirs, but there was no mistaking the recognition in their hearts. This was their child, their flesh and blood.

Eve knelt before him, tears welling in her eyes as she reached out. "How did you…?" she began, but the words caught in her throat.

The boy tilted his head, his innocent gaze meeting hers. "Mama?" he asked softly.

Eve's heart swelled with an emotion she had never known. She had once been a child, but this was different. This was responsibility—the burden as well as the blessing of it. The weight of the knowledge they had gained now pressed even harder, for in this child lay the consequences of their choices. Could they protect him from the same mistakes they had made? Could they teach him to navigate a world so fraught with uncertainty?

Adam stepped forward, his hand resting on Eve's shoulder. "He's our responsibility now," he said gently, his voice filled with a quiet determination. "We'll teach him. We'll give him everything we didn't have."

Eve looked up at him, her heart torn. "But how do we teach him about the world we've created? How do we protect him from the mistakes we have made?"

Adam's gaze softened as he knelt beside her. "We teach him what we know. We show him how to live in this world—not in fear, but with hope. We give him what we can. We build a future, Eve. Together."

As they sat together, their hands resting on the boy, they knew their lives would never be the same. The burden of their choices had become the burden of parenthood; but it was also the opportunity to redeem themselves through love, sacrifice, and growth. This was a new beginning—not just for them, but also the child and world they would make.

EXPLORE THE EMOTIONAL DEPTH OF PARENTHOOD:

By exploring the emotional depth of Adam and Eve as parents, their story takes on a profound dimension as they face the challenges and pressures of raising children in an irrevocably changed world. Their relationship with their children is a journey marked by love, sacrifice, hope, and a struggle with the weight of their own past—a narrative that mirrors the universal experience of parenthood in profound ways.

THE COMPLEXITY OF LOVE AND GUILT

Parenthood is a matter of deep complexity to Adam and Eve. They love their children fiercely, yet this love is shrouded in guilt and regret because their offspring will never know the beauty of Eden. As the first parents in a "fallen" world, they bear a dual responsibility: raising their children with care and teaching them about a world marked by suffering—an inheritance that is no fault of the children.

Duality can be an emotional challenge. They love their children fiercely but also must contend with a sense of loss and guilt. Eve may feel a sense of responsibility, having been the first to be persuaded by the serpent. This makes her love for her children tinged with a sense of responsibility to protect and guide them, even as she feels the blame for bringing them into an imperfect world.

SACRIFICE AS A CONSTANT REALITY

The sacrifices Adam and Eve make for their children are profound. In Eden, they never had to worry about scarcity, hard labour, or safety; yet, in their new reality, everything requires effort and vigilance. Adam is commanded to till the ground so he may provide for his family—a task that requires significant effort, bringing with it inevitable disappointment and exhaustion. Through these sacrifices, he learns humility, patience, and resilience—traits that he wishes to pass on to his children.

Eve also faces the harshness of her new life, especially in childbirth, which is now fraught with pain and risk. This experience helps her to understand life's fragility and teaches her to protectively love. Through the painful yet joyful experience of childbirth, she learns that sacrifice is a crucial component of love—a lesson for her children as they mature.

TEACHING AND NURTURING IN A WORLD WITHOUT INNOCENCE

As their family grows, Adam and Eve's conversations with their children become informed by wisdom as well as caution. They realise that unlike before the Fall, their children must now navigate a world where knowledge of good and evil is necessary for survival. This means their teaching is both practical and moral, encompassing lessons about the world's dangers, making good choices, and resilience.

They teach more than just survival; they try to instil compassion and kindness in their children, hoping that someday these lessons can be used to make the world a better place. But teaching how to be careful and humble also means that they must understand the ease with which one small mistake can lead to suffering. This balance between giving hope and nurturing an awareness that the world is what it is, fosters a delicate growth in Adam and Eve; they develop empathy, patience, and wisdom.

HOPE FOR A BETTER FUTURE

Despite their harsh reality, Adam and Eve continue to nurture a fragile yet potent hope. Their children are seen as the possibility of redemption, building a life that brings beauty and goodness into an otherwise harsh world. Each new milestone in their children's lives—their first steps, first words, first expressions of kindness—gives Adam and Eve a sense that, even in exile, they can still create moments of joy and meaning.

This hope is also a desire for forgiveness and reconciliation. By nurturing their children, they see a way to set things right, guiding them toward values that transcend the failings of one's own self. This hope for a better future becomes a source of strength, helping them endure and invest in their children's growth despite the difficulties they face daily.

FEAR AS A CONSTANT COMPANION

Alongside hope, Adam and Eve are haunted by an abiding sense of fear. They know all too well the consequences of transgression and worry about their children, specifically regarding choices they will make. The knowledge of good and evil has shown them that freedom comes with the potential for harm, and this awareness makes them protective, even overly cautious.

They are especially fearful when they see jealousy, anger, or defiance in their children. Adam and Eve know that unchecked emotions can lead to disastrous choices. This knowledge may prompt them to intervene, trying to instil in their children a sense of humility and respect for one another, while also fearing that they may overstep or stifle their children's growth.

THE PAIN OF LETTING GO AND TRUSTING

As their children grow, Adam and Eve face the inevitable pain of letting go. Despite their desire to protect and guide them, they know that their children must eventually forge their own paths. This means giving them the freedom to make their own choices, even though they understand all too well the dangers of doing so. Letting go requires a profound trust in their children's capacity to learn from life's challenges.

This tension between guidance and independence forces Adam and Eve to trust their children and their own parenting, even in moments of uncertainty. Their journey is one of releasing control while still offering a foundation of love and support, teaching them the importance of resilience, forgiveness, and growth.

THE UNBREAKABLE BOND OF FAMILY AND REDEMPTION

Through all the hardships and heartbreaks, Adam and Eve's bond with their children remains a source of meaning and redemption. Each challenge they face strengthens their love, teaching them that even in a flawed world, the gift of family is a path toward healing and wholeness. Their relationship with their children, marked by both joy and sorrow, teaches them that love is what makes the struggle worthwhile.

This bond may serve as a glimmer of redemption for Adam and Eve, a way of reclaiming the goodness of Eden in small yet profound ways. Watching their children grow, they may view this journey not only as punishment but also an opportunity to create something meaningful and lasting—a family united by love, sacrifice, and hope.

THE TRANSFORMATIVE POWER OF PARENTHOOD

By exploring the emotional depths of parenthood, Adam and Eve's journey is transformed into a narrative of love, sacrifice, and resilience. As parents, they have no choice but to confront their own past, balance hopes and fears, ultimately growing into the teachers and protectors that they are expected to become. In the everyday challenge of bringing up the next generation, they find fleeting beats of joy and redemption—with delicate but lasting hope—such reminders that love and family can endure by forming an alternative path to healing in a fallen world.

Venturing beyond Eden forms a fascinating backdrop to Adam and Eve's story by writing about them as parents and pioneers in a world that is at once familiar and unexpectedly changed. This expanded world-building could enhance stories by adding new dynamics of relationship, moral questions to ponder over, and culture complexities that only serve as a reflection of humanity's first family to the rest of creation.

MEETING OTHER HUMANS: HOW SOCIETY BEGAN TO EXPAND

Adam and Eve's family eventually encounters other humans, symbolizing the spread and diversity of humanity. Such encounters could range from awe and curiosity to conflict and tension. Through these interactions, Adam and Eve get a glimpse into other ways of living—inviting reflection on the significance of community, family, and morality beyond their own experiences.

The presence of other humans creates chances for social interaction and collaboration, but also rivalry and misunderstanding. They may find themselves having to explain their own story of Eden and the knowledge of good and evil—which could be a different kind for these other people. In such encounters, Adam and Eve may even be led to confront the singularity of their origins and how it affects their understanding of human purpose.

DISTINCT CULTURES AND VALUES EMERGING

As they grow up alongside other humans, Adam and Eve's children are exposed to various cultural practices and beliefs that differ from what their parents have taught them. The children encounter different communities with varying rituals, customs, and mythologies that provide a contrast to Adam and Eve's experiences.

This diversity challenges Adam and Eve's beliefs about the world, prompting questions on morality, good and evil, as well as if their experiences in Eden give them unique insight; or whether others can reach their own understanding too. Adam and Eve's children might be drawn to aspects of these other cultures, adding tension as they negotiate which parts of their parents' teachings they will keep and which they might adapt or reject.

NEW RELATIONSHIPS AND THE QUESTION OF ALLEGIANCE

As Adam and Eve's children grow and form friendships, alliances, and even romantic connections outside the family, new questions arise about loyalty, identity, and community. These relationships can test the family's unity, creating tension as Adam and Eve try to balance their protective instincts with allowing their children to create new bonds.

Certain alliances could be beneficial by offering support, trade, and knowledge-sharing opportunities that help Adam and Eve's family to adapt. However, relationships with other groups might also bring rivalries, competition for resources, and power struggles that reveal deeper conflicts. Adam and Eve may face moral and ethical dilemmas in such situations, having to balance their family's well-being against the realities of a growing world with its competing interests.

CONFLICTS WITH OTHER GROUPS: TENSIONS AND TERRITORY

The expansion of the human population results in increasing demand for essential resources such as land, water, and shelter—which sets the stage for territorial disputes. This could potentially create an external source of tension, forcing Adam and Eve into tough decisions regarding new alliances, protection, and survival.

In these struggles, Adam and Eve and their descendants will have no choice but to contemplate challenging questions on leadership, justice, and empathy. As they navigate these disputes, Adam and Eve are called to mediate or even lead, though their authority may be challenged by others who either resist them or resent what they represent. These trials compel them to evaluate themselves and reflect on their values, as well as their sphere of influence in a growing human community.

EXPLORING KNOWLEDGE, TECHNOLOGY, AND PROGRESS

As communities interact, they share knowledge and skills that pave the way for early technological advancements in agriculture. This progress shows human creativity by illustrating the idea that, even outside Eden, humans are able to shape their environment and improve lives.

Adam and Eve face a double-edged sword with this advancement, having to deal with the responsibility that comes from new knowledge. The development of tools, techniques, and structures might echo their own experience with forbidden knowledge, reminding them that progress, while beneficial, can also have unintended consequences. They experience the challenge of teaching their children to find balance, respecting knowledge's power while tempering it with humility and responsibility.

THE IMPACT OF ADAM AND EVE'S STORY: REVERENCE AND RESENTMENT

The story of Eden becomes a foundational myth for Adam and Eve, but reactions to this may vary widely. Some people might regard Adam and Eve with awe or reverence, seeing them as the first humans who were in paradise but exiled. Such reverence could afford Adam and Eve a unique, almost legendary status, with some seeing them as wise guides.

However, others might view Adam and Eve with scepticism or even resentment. Those who have no experience of Eden might see their story as a cautionary tale or a tragic reminder of humanity's limitations. Some might envy their connection to Eden, while others could dismiss them as irrelevant stories that do not pertain to their own lives. These varied responses challenge Adam and Eve's perception of themselves and their legacy as they grapple with what it means to be human without the privilege of paradise.

The Spiritual Legacy and Search for Redemption

Interacting with other groups makes Adam and Eve ponder the spiritual legacy they are leaving behind. As the human population grows, Adam and Eve's children and descendants might become curious about divinity—seeking purpose beyond survival through understanding.

In this pursuit of meaning, early spiritual practices and beliefs might arise—some grounded in Adam and Eve's teachings, others from fresh insights into the world. These practices might include forms of worship, meditation, or reflection that serve as reminders of Eden and aspirations for reconciliation with the divine. As Adam and Eve see their story inspiring these rituals, they gain a sense of the impact they have on the evolving human spirit, even if reconciliation with God the Creator is yet to be achieved.

A CHANGING SENSE OF HOME AND BELONGING

With new people, cultures, and values around them, Adam and Eve might find their sense of "home" shifting. Having left Eden, they have already experienced exile. But as they encounter others and see the growing diversity of human life, they must redefine what it means to belong.

This sense of belonging could be tested as they navigate the complexities of human society, witnessing both its beauty and its flaws. Adam and Eve may find a new sense of home in the relationships they form, not only with each other and their children but with the broader world and humanity. As they go through this process, Adam and Eve might come to understand that the world beyond Eden—though imperfect—has its own potential for paradise, one forged by resilience, unity, and shared human experience.

CONCLUSION: A RICHLY WOVEN HUMAN STORY

The expansion of Adam and Eve's world brings their story into the realm of collective human experience. Through encounters with others, they are drawn into a complex web of relationships, conflicts, cultural exchanges, and spiritual journeys, creating a narrative that mirrors the broader human condition.

These experiences deepen Adam and Eve's role as parents, pioneers, and leaders, inviting them—and their children—to engage with the world in all its beauty and challenge. Their journey in this broader context offers a narrative of growth, adaptation, and the gradual shaping of human identity, exploring what it means to seek paradise not in a place, but within the human spirit.

CHAPTER 9:
The Serpent's Shadow

Years went by in the harsh but fertile land beyond Eden. Adam and Eve's child, whom they named Cain, grew up quickly as children do. He was energetic, and his curiosity was as keen as Eve's had been in her youth. However, Adam noticed a certain novelty in his eyes, a shadow of doubt. It was subtle, but it was there, like a whisper in the back of his mind, urging him to question everything.

Eve noticed it, too. Cain had not only inherited their thirst for knowledge, but also something else—that same kind of restlessness that had driven her to the tree in Eden. Though she wished to protect him from the fallout of their actions, a part of her could not deny that he was one and the same. He seemed fated to struggle with the unknown, to wrestle with concepts of good and evil that had been tasted so long ago by them.

One evening, as they sat around a fire after dinner, Eve watched her son quietly staring into the flames. Adam was sharpening tools with his mind on the task. Eve wanted to believe they had built something meaningful in this new world, yet the guilt of losing Eden still lingered. And now, as Cain began to question, it felt as though the cycle was about to repeat itself.

"Cain?" Eve called gently.

He turned, his young face curious but also distant. "Yes, Mama?"

"What are you thinking about?" she asked, knowing full well that his mind had been wandering into places she could not follow.

Cain's lips parted as if to speak, but then he hesitated. "I was thinking about the serpent," he said quietly. "Why did it want you to eat the fruit?"

Eve's heart clenched. She exchanged a glance with Adam, who had stopped sharpening his tools. Neither of them had expected Cain to ask about the serpent, but it was clear that the questions had already begun. There was no hiding from the past, not for them, and certainly not for their son.

"The serpent was a trickster, Cain," Adam began, his voice measured. "It wanted us to disobey God."

"But why?" Cain pressed. "If it was bad, why did it seem so…right?"

Eve felt a shiver run through her. It was the same question she had asked herself a thousand times, the same question Adam had struggled with in the silence of their lonely days. The serpent had whispered promises of knowledge and power, tempting them with what seemed like the right path. It had been cunning, persuasive, and in many ways, it had opened their eyes to a world they hadn't known existed.

"It showed us things," Eve said slowly. "Things we could not have known otherwise. But with that knowledge came pain, and the world was never the same again."

Cain looked at her for a long moment, then nodded, though his eyes remained troubled.

"The serpent didn't just change you and Papa, did it?" he asked, his voice small. "It changed everything. Didn't it?"

Adam was quiet for a moment, his gaze hardening as he looked at the boy who had become a mirror of their own restless past. Eve's heart sank as the weight of Cain's words settled upon them both.

"Yes," Adam said at last. "It did."

THE SERPENT'S CHARACTER AND LEGACY

The serpent in the Garden of Eden is one of the most enigmatic and complex figures in the story of Adam and Eve. The serpent traditionally represents deception and seduction, which makes it an intriguing character full of opposites. To develop this character, we need to examine its motives and methods as well as the symbolism behind it.

ORIGINS AND NATURE

The serpent is described as the most cunning of all creatures, a trait that sets it apart from the other animals in Eden. Its ability to communicate with Eve implies intelligence and intention beyond that of other creatures. Was its cunning nature an intrinsic quality or a gift bestowed upon the serpent by some higher power? Examining the serpent's origins gives more depth to its persona. Maybe the serpent had a noble role in the garden that devolved into bitterness, jealousy, or corruption.

MOTIVES AND INTENTIONS

The serpent's motives remain ambiguous in the narrative. Is it simply a trickster, enjoying chaos for chaos's sake, or does it have its own twisted philosophical view? Possibly, it perceives the fruit of the Tree of Knowledge as a means to free Adam and Eve from their ignorance—believing knowledge is a greater good than mere obedience. Or perhaps the serpent is just a cog in a greater cosmic machine, executing some plan beyond its comprehension.

METHODS OF TEMPTATION

The serpent's approach to Eve is calculated and strategic. It appeals to her curiosity, her desire for wisdom, and her sense of autonomy. The dialogue reveals its ability to manipulate language and twist truths to serve its purpose. An example of this is when the serpent questions God's command in a way that seeds doubt: "Did God really say you must not eat from any tree in the garden?" This way of asking questions—instead of issuing commands—shows its psychological aptitude.

SYMBOLISM

The serpent symbolises dualities: wisdom and deceit, life and death, freedom and servitude. Its slithering nature reflects its ability to navigate the boundaries between these opposites, embodying both the potential for enlightenment and the danger of hubris. In some readings, the serpent stands for the human struggle with moral ambiguity and the longing to know what should not be known.

THE SERPENT'S ROLE IN ADAM'S TEMPTATION

Expanding the serpent's role to include Adam's temptation adds complexity and depth to its character. After successfully convincing Eve, the serpent has a heated conversation with Adam, to whom it presents a different argument tailored to Adam's doubts and desires. This exchange shows how adaptable the serpent is; it understands human nature deeply—exploiting Adam's fear of being alone, his reliance on Eve, and his latent curiosity about the fruit.

REDEMPTION OR ETERNAL VILLAIN?

Can the serpent change, or is it doomed to stay the same? Its part in the Fall might not mark the end of its tale. The serpent could later reflect on the consequences of its actions, providing a lens through which to explore themes of regret, accountability, and the possibility of redemption. It may want to find a new purpose, an avenue for change reflecting on its decisions and asking if they were influenced by malice or misguided conviction. This inner struggle could lead the serpent to seek a new role—transforming from an agent of chaos into one of restoration. Its journey could mirror humanity's own struggle with guilt and redemption, adding a nuanced layer to its role in the broader narrative.

The serpent, with its promise of knowledge, had forever altered the course of humanity. Its role was not just to tempt—it was to awaken. It was the catalyst that set Adam and Eve on a path of self-awareness and choice, but it was also the beginning of their separation from innocence. While often seen as evil, the serpent was in many ways a necessary force for human development. Without it, they would have remained untested, untouched by the complexities of good and evil.

Yet, that knowledge brought with it the burden of choice: every action having consequences; and understanding—not just possessing—knowledge was peace. The serpent's legacy, then, was not just in the act of temptation, but in the awareness it instilled; an awareness that would continue to shape humanity in ways both dark and light.

Eve had not been wrong to desire knowledge; in fact, it was this very desire that had driven them forward. But in the balance of knowing and living, she and Adam had learned that wisdom without love could become a burden too heavy to bear.

CHAPTER 10:
The First Lessons

As Cain grew, so did the complexities of their life outside Eden. No longer were they just survivors, they were teachers, guides, and parents. They now had to teach Cain about the world, about the consequences of their actions, and about the difficult path ahead.

One evening, as they sat by the fire, Adam and Eve spoke of the lessons they had learned. It was time to pass those lessons on to Cain. It did not take long before they realized that it was harder than they had anticipated. How could they explain the nature of good and evil to a child who had yet to understand the meaning of either?

"Cain," Eve said, calling her son to her side. "Do you remember what we told you about the serpent?"

Cain nodded. "It was bad. It tricked you."

"Yes," Eve said gently. "But it also gave us something we did not have before—awareness. It made us see the world in a new way. It showed us that we are not just creatures of instinct, but humans capable of choice."

Adam looked at his son, his gaze intense. "But with that choice comes re-sponsibility. Every choice you make will change things, sometimes in ways you cannot predict."

Cain looked up at them, his brow furrowed in confusion. "But how do I know what's right?"

Adam smiled softly, though his eyes were filled with a sadness that only time could bring. "You will not always know, Cain. That is the nature of the world we live in. But you will learn. You will make mistakes, and you will grow."

"And we'll be here to guide you," Eve added, her voice steady.

Cain thought for a moment, then asked, "Will I always remember the serpent?"

Eve hesitated. "You will," she said quietly. "But you will also remember the love and the choices you make for yourself. In the end, it is not the serpent that will define you, but the life you build."

ADAM AND EVE'S EARLY PARENTING STRUGGLES AND THEIR ATTEMPTS TO RAISE CAIN

Raising a child in a world without precedent is a monumental challenge; and for Adam and Eve, it is compounded by their recent exile from Eden. They must navigate parenting with no role models, no cultural framework, and only their instincts and limited knowledge to guide them.

THE FIRST CRY

Cain's birth is a moment of both joy and fear. Eve, who names him Cain ("I have gotten a man with the help of the Lord"), sees his arrival as a sign of hope and divine favour. However, the absence of medical knowledge or birthing practices makes the experience harrowing. Adam and Eve must rely on trial and error to care for their infant, learning to interpret his cries, provide nourishment, and protect him from the harshness of their pristine environment.

BALANCING SURVIVAL AND NURTURING

Survival is a constant concern. Adam and Eve must hunt, gather, and build shelter while tending to Cain's needs. This dual burden creates tension between their roles as providers and parents. Eve's bond with Cain may lead her to overprotectiveness, while Adam's focus on survival may cause him to feel disconnected from the child. These dynamics can create moments of misunderstanding and conflict.

TEACHING AND DISCIPLINE

How does one teach a child without books, schools, or societal norms? Adam and Eve must rely on storytelling based on their experiences in Eden and beyond to impart lessons about the world, morality, and their own mistakes. They struggle with the question of discipline—how to correct Cain's behaviour without undue harshness or leniency. Their lack of experience leads to inconsistencies, which Cain may exploit as he grows older.

GUILT AND PROJECTION

Their sense of guilt over their disobedience in Eden influences their parenting. Adam and Eve may project their fears onto Cain, warning him excessively about disobedience while inadvertently passing on their own feelings of shame and regret. This dynamic could shape Cain's personality, planting the seeds for future conflict.

THE STRAIN ON THEIR RELATIONSHIP

Parenting magnifies the existing strains in Adam and Eve's relationship. They may argue over priorities, methods of discipline, and their differing visions for Cain's future. However, these challenges also offer opportunities for growth as they learn to communicate and cooperate more effectively.

THE QUESTION OF FAITH

Raising Cain forces Adam and Eve to grapple with their faith. How do they explain the existence of God the Creator, the garden, and the forbidden fruit to their child? They must decide how much to reveal about their past and how to frame their relationship with God. This decision has profound implications for Cain's worldview and his eventual choices.

CAIN AS THE FIRSTBORN OF A FALLEN WORLD

As the first child born outside of Eden, Cain faces life post-Eden as the first generation; in such a world, the plague of lost innocence. He knows his parents once lived in perfect harmony and were banished for violating God's command. Cain bears the weight of a legacy: separation from paradise and a relationship with God strained to breaking point. He grows up knowing that his parents' actions meant he was born into a world of labour and hardship.

Cain feels more pressure because of his unique status as the firstborn. He must navigate his own feelings about the "curse" of his ancestry while forging his path in a harsh world. This burden might cause resentment, pushing him to question his parents and himself—even God, who stands at the gateway of Eden's return and won't let in anyone from his family.

TENSION BETWEEN KNOWLEDGE AND AMBITION

With knowledge of good and evil inherited, Cain becomes aware of moral complexity at an early age; but craves something more—perhaps a significance or meaning that reflects the perfection of Eden. His ambition could stem from the desire to prove his worth, a sort of recompense for what was lost in the Fall; or an aspiration that he might somehow overcome ancestral shortcomings.

This ambition becomes entwined with his identity. However, as he begins to see the disparity between his ideals and reality, tension grows within him. His desire for divine favour and his own unique relationship with God becomes urgent. However, his awareness of good and evil complicates his choices, leaving him often second-guessing, frustrated, and haunted by self-doubt.

A DEEP DESIRE FOR GOD'S APPROVAL

Cain's offering to God, as recorded in Genesis, can be seen as a pivotal expression of his desire for connection, purpose, and approval. Unlike his brother Abel, who offers a humbler sacrifice, Cain's sacrifice might reflect not only his ambition but his struggle to prove his worth to a God who once dwelled with his parents in Eden.

When God accepted Abel's sacrifice but not his own, Cain felt the sting of rejection. This touches upon his deepest insecurities and fears: that he is unworthy and separated from God in an unbridgeable way. This pain may lead to bitterness and envy, which further fuels a fierce inner struggle that eventually drives him to kill his brother—severing himself even more from his ideals as well. The full story about Cain and Abel will be in the sequel.

STRUGGLE WITH INHERITED GUILT AND ENVY

Cain is haunted not only by his own perceived shortcomings but by a sense of inherited guilt from the original Fall. He is the first to experience sin's impact in both his family dynamic and his relationship with God. As he fights feelings of envy toward Abel, combined with abandonment by God, Cain epitomises the intense—and often destructive—struggle to make peace within a reality dictated by choices that are not his own.

Eden's shadow looms large over Cain, manifesting a smouldering desire to rise above his lineage, yet trapping him further within an endless cycle of resentment and anger. The knowledge of good and evil, inherited from his parents, becomes a source of both insight and torment as he tries to understand his purpose in a world where he feels constantly judged and where nothing seems to measure up to the stories of Eden.

THE MOMENT OF FRACTURE: DRIVEN BY CHOICE AND DESTINY

Cain's eventual decision to kill Abel can be seen as the breaking point in his struggle—a tragic attempt to assert control over a life that feels unfair and incomplete. In that moment, his desire for something greater and his struggle with envy converge. He lashes out at Abel, perhaps feeling that by removing his "rival," he can claim a unique place in God's eyes. However, the act only deepens his isolation, marking him with a lasting separation from both family and God.

After Abel's death, Cain is "marked" and cast out—a symbolic reflection of his inner alienation made literal. His act of violence leaves him exiled not only from his family but from any sense of belonging. As a wanderer, he must confront the full weight of his actions and the consequences of the knowledge of good and evil that has driven him to this point.

THE AMBIGUITY OF CAIN'S LEGACY: WANDERING AND SEARCHING FOR REDEMPTION

Cain's exile turns him into a wanderer, fittingly so for his fragmented self. He has lost his family, his purpose, and his innocence. Yet, in some interpretations, this wandering becomes a kind of search—a quest to find meaning of redemption in a world that seems to have no place for him.

The mark of Cain is traditionally seen as a sign of protection, as God prevents others from taking his life. This mark could be interpreted as a sign of God's mercy; a small reminder that despite his failings, Cain is not entirely forsaken. His journey is one of continual tension between his desire for meaning and his fear of being forever cast out.

CAIN AS A SYMBOL OF THE HUMAN STRUGGLE WITH LEGACY AND IDENTITY

Cain's character can be understood as a symbol of humanity's struggle with inherited guilt, ambition, and the desire for redemption. His journey reflects the human experience of grappling with the past, with moral complexity, and with the need to forge an identity in a world that offers no easy answers. Cain's story is a tragic reminder of how the search for something greater, without the grounding of humility and self-acceptance, can lead to alienation and violence.

Simultaneously, his narrative prompts thoughts about redemption and the ability to transcend one's heritage. Though Cain's exile appears bleak, his mark of protection suggests that even in his wandering, there is hope—a subtle hint that, despite his actions, Cain's journey might hold the potential for transformation and insight.

CONCLUSION: CAIN'S COMPLEX LEGACY

By delving into Cain's struggle with his heritage, we see a portrait of a man caught between knowledge, ambition, and deep-seated longing. His journey, though tragic, sheds light on the complex human search for purpose, acceptance, and reconciliation with one's origins. In Cain, we find the raw human desire to matter, to be understood, and to transcend the limitations of one's past. His story invites reflection on the universal human themes of inheritance, personal choice, and the possibility—though perhaps distant—of finding redemption even in exile.

CHAPTER 11

The Road Less Travelled

Cain had always been curious, that much was undeniable. From the time he could walk, his gaze went out to the wilderness and beyond, to the lands unfamiliar with his parent's small homestead. Adam and Eve had tried to shield him from the harsh realities of the world, but Cain had inherited their desire to understand. He longed to see what lay beyond their small, self-sufficient life.

His questions had only deepened with age. Cain wanted to unravel the mysteries of a vast world; and they were many. He often asked his parents about the stories of Eden, about the garden they had lost, and about the serpent that had forever altered their lives. But the answers were always the same: the garden was gone, and the serpent had tricked them into disobedience. There was little left to say; but Cain's questions kept coming.

One day, Cain decided to leave. It was not rebellion, but something necessary—he could not resist the call of the unknown any longer. The road before him, leading out of the shelter of their home and into the wilderness, beckoned with the same allure that had called to his parents in their youth. He needed to see the world for himself.

He did not tell his parents right away. He could not articulate why he had to leave. How could he put into words what burned inside him—a desire to find something beyond what they had taught him? Was it knowledge? Freedom? Or that gnawing feeling there was something out there, just beyond reach?

The decision weighed heavily on Cain's heart. He knew his parents would worry. But he needed to know. His questions were nagging him, and they had to be answered. So, one evening, as the sun dipped low and once again painted the sky with hues of orange and red, Cain slipped quietly into the woods, taking nothing with him.

A WORLD IN MOTION

Cain's journey through the wilderness was not easy. What Adam and Eve had tamed was but a fraction of the wild world beyond. Here, in the dense forest, the air was thick with the scent of earth and decay. The trees were tall and dark, their roots twisted beneath the earth's surface, making each step treacherous. Despite the difficulties, Cain found an odd exhilaration. He was free. For the first time in his life, he was fully alone, outside the boundaries of his parents' teachings and the rules of their small world.

However, as the days passed, Cain recognized the frailty of his independence. He did not have full knowledge of the skills his parents tried to teach him. He could hunt, but he was not good at it. He could forage, but his knowledge was limited. The world outside his home was a far cry from the protected life he had known.

A MAN FROM AFRICANA

One evening, as he settled down for sleep in a makeshift shelter, he saw figures moving through the trees. Shadows at first, then slowly coming into clearer view. They were not like him. Their skin was darker, their faces older and more weathered, and their eyes held something Cain had never seen before: a knowledge of the world's hardships.

At first, Cain was cautious. His parents had always warned him about strangers, about the dangers of the outside world. But as the figures drew closer, one of them stepped forward—a tall, muscular man with a weathered face and a kind smile. He spoke in a language that Cain found a little difficult to understand, but his tone was warm, and the man's eyes were curious rather than judgmental.

The stranger offered Cain food; and after a brief, cautious exchange, Cain accepted. As they sat around the fire, the man began to tell Cain a story of his own people, of their journey from a far-off land—Africana—to this one. His words were simple, but they carried a depth of experience that Cain had never heard before.

"There are many of us," the man said. "We have wandered through many lands and learned from many things. We, too, have known loss. But we have also known how to survive. There is much the world can teach you if you are willing to listen and learn."

Cain listened intently, drawn in by the stranger's words. This was the first time he had heard of others who had lived outside the shadow of Eden, outside the knowledge his parents had given him. The world in the Garden of the Universe was much larger than he had ever imagined; and as the night deepened, Cain realised that he had just begun to understand the vastness of what lay ahead.

A SEED OF CHANGE

Days went by and Cain stayed with the strangers, absorbing their way of life as he taught them what little he knew. Their lives were simple—different from the life Adam and Eve had built; but no less valuable. They had mastered survival in ways Cain had never considered; and through them, Cain began to see the world not just as a place of danger, but as a place of endless possibility.

Cain learned that the strangers' world was full of hardship but also filled with moments of connection—shared knowledge, shared laughter, and shared hardship. It was a stark contrast to the isolation Cain had grown up with.

One day, as Cain sat by the fire with the stranger who had first approached him, he realized something. The world was not just about surviving or seeking knowledge; it was about finding balance. It was about understanding how all the pieces—knowledge, survival, and community—fit together.

"I've learned something," Cain said, his voice steady but full of wonder. "I have learned that we are all connected. Not just in the way we survive, but in the way we live. Everything we do affects someone else. My parents—they wanted to protect me, but they never told me this. They did not know this."

The stranger—who had earlier told Cain that his name was Daniel—nodded, his eyes filled with quiet understanding. "Your parents gave you something important, Cain. They gave you life. But now it is up to you to learn how to live it."

KEY THEMES IN THIS CHAPTER

Cain's Search for Identity: This chapter focuses on Cain's journey to find his own path, separate from the life his parents had built. His journey reflects the human need to explore the unknown, to seek knowledge, and to challenge the boundaries that have been set for us. Cain's search is a pivotal moment in the story—his first steps into the broader world are symbolic of the individual journey that everyone must undertake to discover their purpose.

The Larger World Beyond Eden: As Cain ventures into the wilderness and encounters more strangers, the world expands. The narrative moves from the isolated family dynamics of Adam and Eve's home to a broader exploration of human connection. Cain's meeting with the strangers illustrates the variety of human experience; and how knowledge, survival, and community intersect.

Balance and Community: Cain's reflections about connection emphasize the theme of balance—between knowledge and wisdom, independence and community. The strangers teach him that life isn't just about survival or knowledge, but about understanding how to live in harmony with others. It is a lesson in interdependence, one that Cain will carry with him as he navigates the complexities of life outside Eden.

Further Exploration of Cain's Transformation: As Cain grows in this unique environment, he will struggle with the tension between his parents' teachings and the broader knowledge he is gaining. This internal conflict will play a significant role in shaping his character and his future choices.

Introducing Larger Conflicts: The broader world beyond Eden will become more complex as Cain begins to encounter diverse groups of people, each with their own ideas of survival, power, and community. These interactions will shape his understanding of the world and drive the narrative toward greater conflicts.

Eve and Adam's Response to Cain's Departure: As Cain ventures deeper into the world, the tension between freedom and protection will continue to challenge Adam and Eve. Their response to Cain's journey will add emotional depth to their relationship and reflect the broader theme of parental responsibility.

CHAPTER 12:
The Empty Space Between Them

Days passed into weeks, then weeks became months. Adam and Eve continued their tasks with steady hands, but heavy hearts. Without Cain, the days stretched longer than anticipated. Their home was silent, no longer the peaceful quiet it had once been; even the rhythm of the seasons mocked them now.

Initially, Adam tried to distract himself with duties—tending the fields, repairing shelter, hunting, and gathering. But under it all was a quiet sorrow. Losing Eden had been tough, but this felt different. It was not just the garden that they lost—it was the innocence of their child too. Cain was gone; and though Adam knew this was a part of growing up, he could not shake off the feeling that somehow, they had failed him.

Eve felt it too—an ache in her chest. She often spent hours looking into the distance, thinking about Cain and his exploration of the world. She had given him life, and in turn the freedom to find his own path. Now it was that same freedom that felt like a silent accusation. Had her offering been enough? Were they, as parents, able to prepare him for the harshness beyond their world?

She frequently walked to the edge of their land, gazing into the wilderness, hoping and praying Cain would find his way back. She had no words for the grief that was in her heart, but there was a deep knowledge within her that Cain's journey had just begun, and there was no turning back.

A LETTER UNWRITTEN

One evening, as the sun set in a burst of color over the horizon, Eve sat quietly on the stone steps outside their shelter. Adam had gone to sleep early, his exhaustion from the day's labour catching up with him. But Eve could not rest. She found herself thinking about Cain—wondering where he was, what he was learning, and if he thought of them at all.

She held a small piece of parchment and a quill in her hand. Years had passed since she last wrote anything, not since before the Fall, when she learned how to turn words into a song. It seemed like yesterday when she heard the bird singing…

One early morning, a soft mist enveloped the garden as dew still clung to leaves. The air carried a faint cool sweetness of flowers. Eve walked quietly on the soft grass, her bare feet brushing against it. She was drawn to a familiar apple tree; its boughs weighted with fruit that glinted at the first light of morning.

She sat down under it, resting her back against its smooth trunk. Closing her eyes for a while, she heard the music of Eden—rustling leaves, a distant stream's babble and insects softly buzzing in wakeful greeting.

Suddenly, a clear and melodic tune then drifted from a voice coming from above her. Startled, she looked up to see a small and delicate bird sitting on a nearby branch. The bird—a dove—had become her constant companion. As it sang, its feathers showed shades of blue and gold; the sound was clear and reached deep into Eve's consciousness.

Wonder touched her heart. She had heard birds sing before, but this morning was different. The song the dove was singing felt like a story. She watched the bird breathing each note, amazed at how such a small creature could make something so beautiful. The question arose in her head, softly at first and then pressing:

"How can I, too, sing like this?" she asked the bird.

For the first time, Eve wanted something that wasn't freely given. She had used her voice to speak words, share laughter, and tell Adam about love; but never in music had she tried. The bird's song stirred within her a desire to imitate, learn, and create beauty with her own voice.

Hesitantly, she attempted to sing the words she was going to share with Adam. Her voice came out soft and melodic:

Love is like a burning Flame
Or a brand-new running game
That's difficult to handle.
But when it is treated right,
Love can become a candle
That brightens someone's night.
When it flickers like a dove,
It seems like it can't survive.
The Flame of a budding Love
Can always remain alive!
It needs lots of tenderness,
Tolerance, and constant care.
Nurtured with steady kindness,
Love can drive away your fears,
Though lying dull and tender,
Challenged by some bitter pain.
It stirs in its own embers
And rises to life again!

The bird paused, cocked its head, as if listening. Emboldened, Eve continued to sing, her notes weaving into the air—imperfect, but full of hope. The bird responded with a trill; and for a brief, magical moment, it felt as though they were speaking to each other—two creatures from different worlds, bound by the universal language of music.

This was more than curiosity. It was the first hint of creativity stirring within her—the desire to shape her own beauty, to add her voice to the garden's song. And though she did not know it yet, this yearning for more—for knowledge, for expression—would one day lead her toward choices that would alter everything.

When the dove saw Adam moving closer, it flew off. Eve was disappointed. Then her mind raced back to when Cain was born. She remembered the day she lay beside Adam, with Cain resting between them. The child slept soundly, his tiny chest rising and falling in rhythmic peace. Adam, however, remained still, his gaze distant, his mind elsewhere.

She knew his thoughts. She had seen the weight he carried—his worry for their survival, for the unknown future ahead. She reached for his hand, threading her fingers through his.

"Adam," she whispered. "Look at him."

Adam's eyes flickered to the child, to the small, perfect life they had created. Eve smiled; her voice was steady as she said to Adam:

> Through weary toil, through aching cries,
> A child is born before my eyes.
> From dust we came, yet now I see,
> New life has sprung through you and me.

Adam exhaled, the tension in his shoulders loosening. He turned to her, pressing his forehead against hers. In that moment, there were no questions, no burdens—only them, and the life they had brought into the world...

But tonight, her heart was heavy because she missed her son. Then, she began to write, not knowing if the letter would be for Cain—or perhaps for herself.

My dear son, Cain,

I do not know where you are tonight or what the world looks like through your eyes. Still, I hope you can understand now why we did what we did. The world beyond our home is not as kind as the garden we once had. It may bring pain, but it is filled with fleeting moments of grace as well. I hope you will find those moments, even when they seem fleeting. I hope you will remember the love we gave you and carry that with you wherever your journey takes in this vast world. And if you should ever feel lost, or afraid, remember that you are always welcome here, with us.

With all my heart,

Your mother, Eve

Eve paused, the quill hovering over the page. She was not sure if she would ever actually send it. There was nowhere to send it, no means of reaching Cain again. However, writing it out felt like a small act of hope—something she could hold onto while everything else slipped away.

ADAM'S BURDEN

The days following Cain's departure were some of the hardest Adam had ever known. He worked tirelessly, his body moving through the motions of survival, but his mind was consumed with worry. He feared Cain might have gone too far and not returned. A part of him had wanted to hold Cain close, keeping him safe from the pain of the world. But deep down, Adam knew that this was not his path to decide. Cain had grown, and the need for independence was something Adam had come to accept, even if it made him feel powerless.

One night, Adam sat on a large rock outside their shelter, staring at the moon. Eve had retired early; her own thoughts weighed heavily on her mind. Sitting quietly, Adam's emotions were a tangled web of love, fear, and guilt. He thought of Cain, his son, and the path he had chosen to walk. Had they prepared him enough? Had they given him the strength to endure the hardships of the world? Or had they simply sent him out into the unknown with nothing but their love and hope?

Adam closed his eyes, remembering the early days in Eden. The world had seemed so full of promise then. Everything had been simple. If they had never eaten the fruit, if they had never disobeyed, would Cain still be with them? Would they have retained their innocence and home?

There were no answers. In the silence of night, Adam realised something: He could not control the world. He could not control what happened to Cain. But he could love him. He had to trust that, wherever Cain was, he would find his way just as Adam had done in the wilderness of their new life.

A LETTER TO HIS SON

Later that night, as the winds howled outside their shelter, Adam took a deep breath and sat down to write. They both had letters to send, or at least—Adam did too, to Cain. As Adam sat under the sprawling branches of an ancient tree, he held a small parchment in his hands. The words he had just written were filled with love, regret, and hope for his son Cain. Adam's heart was heavy, but he knew he had to try reaching out to his son.

> My dear son, Cain,
>
> If you ever read this, just know that we always think of you. We had to let you go because we know you must find your own way in this world. You are not just our son, but someone who will shape the future in ways we cannot yet understand. We do not know what the world will teach you, but we hope it will teach you wisdom, kindness, and strength. We hope you will carry on the lessons we have taught you and build something greater than what exists here. The land feels emptier without you, and your absence has carved an ache in my soul. I know the burden you carry is immense, and for that, I am deeply sorry. But, my son, I ask that you find it in your heart to remember the good that still exists in this vast Garden of the Universe.
>
> With love and hope,
>
> Your father, Adam.

Adam folded the parchment carefully, then opened it again. He stared at the letter, his brow furrowed. "How can I get this to him?" he muttered to himself. He glanced around the clearing, hoping for inspiration. That was when he noticed a pigeon perched nearby, preening its feathers.

Adam's lips curled into a hesitant smile. He rose and approached the bird cautiously. "Hello, little one," he said softly. The pigeon tilted its head, its beady eyes studying him curiously.

"I have a favour to ask," Adam began, kneeling before the bird. "My son is far away, and I have no way to reach him. But you…you can fly. Will you help me?"

The pigeon let out a soft coo, almost as if considering his words. Adam chuckled; half amused at himself. "What am I doing? Talking to a bird. But still, you're here, and I—"

"What is it you need?" a voice interrupted. Adam froze, his eyes widening. The pigeon's head bobbed slightly as it spoke, its voice calm and melodic.

"You…you can understand me?" Adam stammered.

"Of course," the pigeon replied. "Many creatures of this world listen and understand, though few choose to speak."

Adam sat back, awe replacing his initial shock. "I need your help to deliver this letter to my son. He's far away, and I don't know where. But if you could find him…"

The pigeon fluffed its feathers. "A heavy task, but not impossible. Describe him to me."

Adam's voice wavered with emotion. "He's strong, with a face much like mine but younger. His eyes are sharp, often clouded with anger. He left to wander the earth…and I fear he's alone, consumed by guilt."

The pigeon nodded. "I will do my best to find him. Attach your letter, and I will carry it."

Tears filled Adam's eyes as he gently tied the parchment to the pigeon's neck with a strip of bark. "Thank you," he whispered. "Thank you for giving me hope."

The pigeon cooed softly, then spread its wings. Adam stepped back, watching as the bird took flight, its small form disappearing into the vast sky.

"Birds are so amazing," Adam mused as he remembered when Eve told him how a bird taught her how to sing…

One day, as he was roaming the grounds, he heard Eve singing. Eve didn't realize Adam was near enough to hear her sing. When his voice broke the gentle stillness, she turned around in surprise.

"That's a lovely song," he said, his eyes warm with admiration.

Eve blushed. "You heard me?"

"How did you learn to sing like that?" Adam asked, stepping closer.

"Do you remember the dove I named Evelene? I heard her singing one morning and asked if she could teach me. She did," Eve explained, her face glowing with the memory.

Adam smiled. "I wish I could sing the words I have in my heart for you."

Eve reached for his hand. "Then speak the words to me as you always do. I can't wait to hear what you hold inside." As she led Adam towards the river, Adam began to speak…

Even when the cold winds blow,
And my spirit sinks so low,
I want you always to know—
I will forever love you.

When loneliness fills my day,
And time drifts slowly away,
Even when skies turn gray—
My love will still be true.

I don't count the hours apart,
For you are etched in my heart.
My joy depends, from the start,
On every moment with you.

Nothing can break this bond,
Nor pull my heart from beyond.
Through storms or sunny skies,
I will love you—always.

Their eyes met, and for a moment, the beauty of the garden around them faded, leaving only the melody of their hearts intertwined…

For the first time in days, Adam felt a glimmer of peace. He didn't know if the letter would reach Cain, but the act of trying gave him solace. As he turned to walk back to Eve, he whispered a silent prayer for the bird's safe journey and for his son's heart to find healing.

KEY THEMES IN THIS CHAPTER

Parental Love and Letting Go: Adam and Eve's emotional turmoil reveals the deep, often painful process of letting go of their child. They love Cain unconditionally, but they also understand that his journey is one he must take alone. The chapter explores the complexity of love and the tension between protecting and allowing freedom.

The Burden of Guilt and Hope: Both Adam and Eve wrestle with guilt, wondering if they did enough to prepare Cain for the world outside or whether they had failed him. Yet they remain hopeful. They hope that Cain will find his way, learn from his experiences, and return stronger than before. This internal conflict forms the emotional backbone of the chapter.

The Silent Strength of the Parent's Heart: In the absence of their son, both Adam and Eve find a quiet strength in their love. It is a strength born from the acceptance that their child's journey is his own, but it is also a strength in knowing that love transcends distance and time.

NEXT STEPS FOR THE STORY

Cain's Growth in the Broader World: As Cain continues his journey, he will begin to encounter more diverse groups of people and face challenges that test his understanding of survival, community, and the knowledge he has gained. These experiences will shape him into a more complex figure.

Eve and Adam's Reconciliation with the Past: Adam and Eve will continue to grapple with the emotional toll of Cain's departure. Their letters, sent or not, will function as catalysts for their own inner reconciliation. The journey of letting go will continue to evolve as they find new ways to cope with their changing relationship with Cain.

The Broader Impact of Cain's Journey: Cain's departure marks a significant turning point in the story. As he moves further away, the impact of his choices will ripple through the world around him, influencing others and shifting the family dynamic in unexpected ways.

CHAPTER 13:
The Healing of the Heart

Time passed differently after Cain left. Days didn't stretch on; they carried more weight, meaning that each day Adam and Eve spent without their son was imbued with a depth of significance they'd never known. Their life's routine had changed; the absence of the boy whom they love, care for, and guided through life deeply—had irrevocably altered it. Yet in this absence, there was room for something new to emerge—a different kind of presence.

Adam, usually the dependable one, started to transform. The burden of responsibility, once solely his, had grown to also encompass healing spiritually. Without Cain by his side, Adam walked a path of reflection and reconciliation with himself—and all the choices he had made both within Eden and since their Fall from grace.

He often recalled that moment—the moment he bit into the fruit, exchanging innocence for knowledge. Blaming Eve was easy; perhaps he still did at heart. But now his reflection took a different turn. He thought about so many different choices he could have made and wondered if he had failed Cain in passing on the wisdom to face this world with strength.

The days dragged on, but Adam found peace in his quiet labours. He repaired their shelter, gathered firewood, and made sure the crops were growing. But the work no longer felt like a burden—it was, in its own way, a form of prayer. As he worked, his mind wandered to Cain and Eve; that silent space between them still filled with grief.

Eve has also changed since Cain left, though her transformation was subtler and less visible. She tended to the land every day, but her heart was with

Cain far away. It was not just the loss of their son—it was also the loss of something within herself. Before Cain left, Eve was the nurturer and caregiver; she protected him. But now she was learning to let go, to allow her child the space to grow. She found this deeply painful but was beginning to accept that loving someone did not always mean keeping them close—it often meant letting go with trust.

Every evening after the day's work was done, Eve sat on the same stone steps where she had written her letter to Cain. The stars shone brightly above her, as they always had; and in the vastness of the night sky, Eve began to feel a different kind of peace. It was as though the universe, in its unfathomable vastness, was reminding her that the world was bigger than her sorrow. She did not know what the future held for her son—but had to trust that his choices were his, and whatever path he chose, he did not walk alone.

THE WISDOM OF LETTING GO

One evening, as the cool air wrapped around them and the fire flickered low, Eve and Adam sat together in silence. They had filled the space between them with the sound of their grief, but now it stretched before them in a way that invited healing. Their sparse conversation was imbued with an unspoken understanding. Neither mentioned Cain's departure—there was no need. Silence had become their shared language.

Eve looked at Adam, and her eyes grew soft, filled with a quiet strength.

"Do you think we will ever see him again?" she asked in a voice barely loud enough to hear.

Adam exhaled deeply, gazing at the stars—the same stars that had witnessed his time in Eden, and now looked down upon his son. "I don't know," he replied, his voice steady.

"But I know he is out there, learning what needs to be learned. The world is vast, Eve, and his journey is just beginning. We gave him life, but we cannot choose his path."

Eve nodded, burdened yet liberated. Finally, after all the time since Cain left them, she found some peace. It was not that her sorrow was gone, or that her longing for Cain had disappeared. Instead, she realised love was not about holding on but sometimes, letting go.

Then she began to hum a song as the thought of Cain enveloped them:

O Cain, my son, my greatest prize,
I see the world within your eyes.
No Eden's walls, no garden bright,
Yet love still shines, a guiding light.
Though sorrow shaped the path we tread,
Hope is born where fears have bled.
For in your breath, so soft and true,
A mother's love is made anew.

FINDING PURPOSE IN PAIN

In the months that followed, Adam and Eve continued their lives, but something had shifted within them. Adam started seeing the land not as a place of punishment, but as one full of possibility. He no longer saw their lives as mere survival, but rather an opportunity to thrive. The soil they worked with, the shelter they built, the food they grew—all of it became an act of love. Through these actions, Adam began to heal.

Eve too had started to find new ways of nurturing. Her work in the fields became more attuned to the seasons as she gained surer hands tending plants and animals. She no longer viewed her labour as a means of penance, but rather, as an offering—a gift to the earth, herself, and the world around her.

In this quiet healing space, Adam and Eve both began to see that the world was not just a mirror of their pain, but one of transformation. They had been given a second chance, one not only to survive but to build. Even though Eden was no more, they could find meaning from its ashes—and their son's absence would be honoured through the way they lived.

The lessons of their past would remain with them, but they would not define their future. Instead, it would be defined by the love they carried for one another, for Cain, and for the world that had allowed them to begin anew.

As Cain continues his journey, he will encounter new challenges and individuals, expanding his understanding of himself and the world around him. His journey is one of discovery, both external and internal.

CONTINUED EMOTIONAL GROWTH OF ADAM AND EVE

Adam and Eve's spiritual growth will persist as they deal with their past and move forward to create a meaningful future. They will learn more about themselves, their relationship with each other, and the impact of Cain's absence.

SETTING THE STAGE FOR NEW RELATIONSHIPS

Cain's journey will bring him into contact with new characters who may sometimes challenge his beliefs, while others could offer insights on survival, love, and loss. These encounters will further shape his understanding of who he is and who he is becoming.

CHAPTER 14:
The Deepening of the Soul

As time went by, Adam and Eve lived their lives under the shadow of Cain's absence. They never stopped wanting their son back, but that longing had slowly worked its way into a place they could manage—no longer at the forefront of every thought or action. They had learned to carry it like a heavy stone—acknowledged, yet not dictating each step in life. In time, they started to navigate the wilderness of their grief, slowly forging a new connection with each other and the world around them, both emotionally and spiritually.

Adam began to introspect in a way he had not previously. Physical labour was the great refuge, using his energy productively, but now there was something deeper that called to him. The questions about the Fall and his choices that had once plagued him were still there. But they had shifted and morphed into something else: Questions on the nature of life after loss. What was life without paradise? What is the meaning of existence in a world full of uncertainty and pain?

In those quiet hours, after the day's work was done and the earth slept under a night sky, Adam began to grapple deeply with questions of his own existence. He had no answers, but the questions themselves began to shape him, filling the silence between him and Eve with a new kind of understanding. Eve, too, embarked on her own spiritual quest—one defined by both the softness of her nurturing spirit and hardness of their present world.

EVE'S TRANSFORMATION

Eve's transformation was quieter and more intuitive. Adam found introspection through words and labour, whereas Eve connected to it by the land. She had always been attuned to nature, but now, in the absence of Cain, she began to understand it in a new way. The plants she tended, the animals she nurtured, all of it began to feel like a reflection of her own inner life. She saw herself not as a mother alone, but as a protector of life and guardian of growth.

In the mornings, she would walk the fields, her fingers brushing the earth as she worked. The soil had become her teacher. In its depths, she found the rhythm of life: birth and growth, decay, and renewal. There was no finality in nature. Everything that died made room for something new. This lesson—one she had never understood in Eden when all was perfect and unchanging—began to connect with her. Here, in this flawed world, she found beauty within the imperfections. Amid the cycles of life and death, she found hope.

One morning, as Eve knelt beside a small plant she had been tending for weeks, her hands in the earth, she had an epiphany. Her grief for Cain had not disappeared, but it had been transformed. She had let him go, but in doing so, she had learned to live fully in the present. The pain was still there, but it no longer defined her. She could love Cain without needing to possess him. She could let him go, and in that act, she could create space for herself, for Adam, and for the future that lay ahead.

ADAM AND EVE TOGETHER

Over the past months, Adam and Eve's quiet strength had been growing into something tangible in their shared moments. Their relationship had gained a depth it previously lacked; they communicated silently with one another, beyond words. They no longer needed to speak constantly; their presence was enough. They were marked by the journey of loss, but also shaped in ways that had not been anticipated.

One evening, as they sat by the fire, Adam reached for Eve's hand, and for the first time in months, he felt the weight of her touch—not as a burden—but as a source of peace. He looked at her and saw the woman she had become—the woman who had walked beside him through the Fall, through their expulsion, and now, through this new chapter of their lives. She was not the same Eve he had known before, and neither was he the same Adam.

"You've changed," Adam said softly, his voice filled with wonder.

Eve smiled, her eyes soft with understanding. "We've both changed. The world has changed us."

Adam nodded, his thoughts returning to their son. "I hope he's learning. I hope he's finding his way in this world."

Eve's voice was gentle, but resolute. "He is. And we must trust that whatever happens, we gave him what we could. The rest is his journey now."

For a moment, they sat in silence, the weight of their words hanging in the air between them. It was not a silence filled with sorrow, but one filled with peace. They had come to a place of acceptance, of understanding. Their son was out there in the world, and though they could not protect him from everything, they could send him forward with love, with hope, and with faith that he would find his path.

CHAPTER 15:
The Unseen Journey

As the years passed, Adam and Eve continued to work the land and live their lives in the aftermath of the Fall. However, something profound had shifted between them. No longer were they merely two souls bound by shared loss; they had become companions in the deepest sense of the word, partners in the unfolding story of humanity.

There were still moments of grief—fleeting moments, sometimes unbidden, when memories of their son, Cain, would flood their hearts. But those moments, while still painful, had become a part of their emotional landscape, woven into the fabric of their lives. They did not deny the sorrow, but they no longer allowed it to dominate their existence.

Instead, their love for one another had deepened. They had become aware of each other in ways they had not been before. There was a quiet wisdom in their gaze now; an understanding that came not from words, but from the shared experience of life after paradise. Their conversations were fewer, but more meaningful. Every glance held an unspoken connection, every touch was a reaffirmation of the bond they shared.

One evening, as Adam sat by the fire, his weathered hands resting on his knees, Eve sat beside him, close enough that their shoulders brushed. The moonlight danced across their face, casting fleeting shadows and fleeting glimpses of the lives they had lived. The silence between them was not filled with the weight of unspoken words, but rather with the comfort of knowing one another so deeply.

"I sometimes think of the world we could have had," Eve said, her voice low but not sad. "The world we could have built in Eden, if only we had not eaten the fruit."

Adam turned to her, his brow furrowed for a moment. "I don't think I regret our choices," he replied slowly. "Regret does not change the past. It only robs us of the future."

Eve looked at him, her eyes soft. "Then what do we have now, Adam?"

"We have each other," he said simply. "We have this life, and we have the chance to make it something good. A world that is imperfect, yes, but still full of possibilities."

Eve nodded, her gaze turning back toward the horizon, where the last light of the moon was fading into the night. "I have learned that sometimes, the brokenness is what makes us stronger. If we had not fallen, if we had not lost everything, we would never have known how to rebuild."

Adam smiled at her, his expression filled with quiet admiration. "You are right. We have learned to grow in the face of loss. And it is in that growth that we find purpose."

THE HEALING POWER OF MEMORY

While their bond has deepened, Adam and Eve's emotional landscape has also been shaped by memory. Memory was both a gift and a curse—a way to keep their son alive in their hearts, but also a reminder of the paradise they had lost. In their darkest moments, the memory of Eden, of innocence, threatened to consume them. But as time passed, memory became less of a burden and more of a guiding force.

Adam began to understand that memory wasn't just about holding on to the past—it was about understanding how the past had shaped them. Every scar, every hardship, every loss, was a part of their journey, and they could no longer see themselves as mere victims of the Fall. Instead, they began to see themselves as pioneers of a new kind of life. They had been given a second chance—a chance to redefine what it meant to be human.

Eve, too, found peace in memory. She began to see the garden in her mind, not as a place of failure but as a symbol of possibility. She understood now that Eden had been a beginning, but not an end. She no longer saw her Fall as a fall from grace, but as a necessary part of the human experience—a step in the evolution of the soul.

The memory of their son was bittersweet, but it was also a reminder that love never dies. Cain's journey had taken him far from them, but in their hearts, he remained. The love they had for him transcended distance, time, and circumstance. And though they did not know where his path would lead, they trusted that he would find his way.

A NEW BEGINNING

As time wore on, Adam and Eve began to sense a new beginning stirring within them. Their land, once a place of harsh survival, had become a place of growth. The crops they had once struggled to nurture were now abundant. The animals they had tended to, once wary and wild, had become accustomed to their presence. The earth had accepted them, not as rulers, but as partners. In this new world, they were not in control, but they were caretakers. And in their care, they found meaning.

It was in this time of quiet flourishing that Adam and Eve realised that the world beyond their immediate circle was beginning to change as well. New creatures appeared on the horizon—wanderers from the far-off places of the world they had once known in Eden, and yet different. The world was larger than they had imagined. Their lives had been small, confined to the boundaries of their garden, but the greater world had always been out there, waiting for them to discover it.

Eve, with her quiet wisdom, understood this change before Adam did. "We cannot keep the world at arm's length forever, Adam. We must face the future, and we must trust that the lessons we have learned will be enough."

Adam took her hand, his heart full of the quiet peace he had found in their shared journey.

CHAPTER 16

Stepping into the Unknown

The quiet rhythm of Adam and Eve's days had settled into a peaceful pattern. But as the months passed, a subtle shift began to stir in the air. It seemed that it was time for them to move beyond their established boundaries and start a new phase in their lives.

The land had given them all it could, and they had learned its secrets. Their hands had tilled the soil, and their hearts had healed in the quiet communion with nature. Yet there was a sense that their journey was not yet complete—that there was more to the world than the small corner of it they had occupied for so long. It was as though they were being called to step into the wider world, to reconnect with the larger tapestry of life that stretched beyond the familiar horizon.

It was Eve who first spoke of it. One evening, as the sun dipped below the edge of the earth, casting a golden light across the fields, she turned to Adam, her voice calm but filled with a quiet urgency.

"We cannot stay here forever," she said. "The world is calling to us."

Adam looked at her, his brow furrowing in thought. "We have built a life here. We have made this place ours."

Eve nodded. "But we have also been here long enough to know that there is more to learn. More to discover. The world is bigger than this."

Adam's gaze followed hers, taking in the wide expanse of the land. For the first time, he saw it as a whole—vast and full of possibilities. The trees, the hills, the rivers—they had always been a part of his existence. But now, they seemed to stretch out before him, beckoning him into the unknown.

"We've learned to live with the land," Adam said, a smile playing on his lips. "But you are right. There is more for us to learn."

A NEW HORIZON

And so, after much deliberation and quiet conversation, Adam and Eve decided to leave the comfort of their established home. They gathered what little they could carry—seeds, tools, and remnants of their life in Eden— and set out toward the unknown, just as their son did. The decision was not without trepidation; there were still remnants of fear, of uncertainty. The world beyond the garden was vast and unpredictable. But they had both grown strong in ways they had not been before. They were no longer defined by their past mistakes but by the choices they had made to move forward, to rebuild, and to grow.

Their journey took them through landscapes they had never encountered— tall forests, rugged mountains, and vast plains. It was a world that felt raw, untamed, and full of potential. With every step, they discovered new wonders, new creatures, new ways of living. The world was alive in ways they had not understood before. It was both beautiful and harsh, full of contrasts. And with every new challenge, they grew more confident in their ability to navigate this larger world together.

Eve found herself marvelling at the ways nature revealed its strength in new forms. She had always been connected to the earth, but now, in its expansive form, she saw its cycles more clearly—how life and death were intertwined, how even in destruction, there was always the possibility of renewal. She had learned that there was no real beginning or end, only an ongoing journey of transformation. The trees that fell would give way to new ones. The fields that grew barren would be fertilised by their own decay.

Adam, too, felt a deeper connection to the world than he had before. He was no longer just a man who had been banished from Eden—he was a part of this new world, this evolving story. The lessons of their Fall had shaped him, and he saw the world not just as a place to survive, but as a place to understand, to learn, and to create. He knew that the land could be harsh, but it also had the potential to be kind, if one knew how to collaborate with it. The patience he had once learned in Eden had only deepened in this new environment.

Together, they began to shape a new life. It wasn't easy—there were days when the challenges felt insurmountable—but each trial strengthened their resolve. And with each passing day, they began to see that their journey was not just about survival. It was about creation, about shaping something meaningful out of the brokenness of their past. It was about a long and winding road that could lead them to their son!

CHAPTER 17:

Cain's Path of Self-Discovery

THE DESIRE FOR SOMETHING MORE

During his teenage years, Cain's childhood restlessness turned into an intense longing for purpose. He couldn't rely on the limited scope of his parents' knowledge or belief anymore. Cain craved something that would explain and resolve all those questions haunting him since childhood. Why was he alive—and not just subsisting in fields, existing within what they'd made? Is life just about surviving, or is there something more?

He would often observe his parents working the land, caring for the earth and its creatures. It was a simple life, and one that brought contentment to many people—but never sated the deeper yearning within. His mind was swirling with complicated thoughts: questions of good and evil, creation and destruction, life and death—concepts that felt abstract in the world his parents had constructed but were very real in the questions Cain grappled with daily.

Sometimes, Cain found himself torn between the world of his parents and this growing sense that there was something else—something beyond a life of farming, tending to animals, or working in the earth. The more he thought about it, the more he realized that the answers his parents had offered seemed too simple, too constrained by the limitations of the world they had known. The deeper questions of life were not being answered here. Cain realised within him, his future would not be part of the world his parents had built—instead, it lay somewhere else beyond their familiar horizons.

THE BREAKING POINT: A FATEFUL DECISION

The tension between Cain's need for independence and his parents' attempts to guide him came to a head one evening. It was the beginning of spring, and Adam was preparing the fields for planting. Eve had been in the garden, tending to their small collection of plants, her quiet nature a balm to Cain's troubled soul. But for the first time in a while, Cain felt an overwhelming urge to leave. The walls of their home—the world his parents had made—were closing in on him.

He had spent the day in silence, listening to his parents' talk of crops and animals. But nothing they said seemed to ease the disquiet in his heart. At dinner that evening, he stood up abruptly, startling his parents.

"I'm leaving," he said, his voice firm, though there was a hint of uncertainty.

Adam looked up, his brow furrowing with concern. "Where will you go, Cain? You can't just leave."

"I need to find something," Cain replied, his voice quieter now. "I need to understand what I'm meant to do. I cannot stay here any longer."

Eve, seeing the conflict in her son's eyes, stood silently, her heart heavy with the knowledge that this day would come. She had always known that Cain's path would not be the same as Adam's. She reached out to him, her voice gentle. "Cain, you do not have to go. We can help you, guide you."

But Cain shook his head. "No, Mother. I need to find my own way."

With that, Cain turned and left, walking into the night, leaving his parents behind.

THE FIRST STEPS INTO THE UNKNOWN

Cain's departure marked a pivotal moment in his life. He always felt something was missing despite the life provided by his parents, but only by leaving them behind did he begin to understand the weight of his decision. He was stepping into uncharted waters, both spiritually and geographically.

The world beyond their home was vast and unfamiliar. Adam and Eve had made a life in the peaceful countryside, but this was an untamed wilderness filled with unknowns. Thick forests and towering mountains extended as far as the eyes could see, forming a new kind of starkness that Cain had never been aware of. Yet it was there, in that wilderness, that he started seeking answers to his questions.

As the days went by, Cain met different peoples living off land in several ways—some nomadic, others having established settlements. He discovered that there were countless perspectives on life and interpretations of the world. But every new meeting only added to Cain's sense of alienation. Even with all the people he was meeting, something still felt absent to him. The answers to his questions remained elusive.

During one of these interactions, Cain met a travelling merchant who spoke of a faraway land—a place where knowledge and wisdom could be gained, where people had gone beyond mere survival to seek the mysteries of existence. The merchant spoke of a great city, where people lived in harmony with each other and with the world around them, a place where one could find the deeper truths of life.

Cain listened intently, feeling hopeful for the first time in his life. He could find what he was looking for in that distant land. The merchant informed him that the journey would be long and arduous, but those who pursued wisdom were rewarded beyond their imagination. For Cain, this was the sign he had been waiting for—a direction. He had found his next step.

THE DESIRE FOR KNOWLEDGE AND SELF-DISCOVERY

Cain's restlessness and his decision to leave his parents reflect the deep human desire for self-discovery and understanding. His quest for something beyond the known is a recurring theme in coming-of-age stories, in which to find one's true self, an individual must leave behind what's familiar. Cain's decision to leave marks a significant step toward adulthood and independence. Cain's internal struggle with staying in the familiar world of his parents or venturing into the unknown is a tension many people face as they move from childhood to adulthood, confronting and conquering daunting yet necessary unknowns.

This theme of searching for purpose in the wider world is central to his journey and reflects the common human experience of outgrowing the constraints of familial expectations to forge one's own identity.

But with this new beginning came new challenges. As Cain grew, so did his emotional complexity. He inherited curiosity from his mother, Eve, but there was also a kind of restlessness in him—a need to prove himself and stand out. Adam noticed this trait in him from an early age and related to it—he remembered his own struggles long ago when temptation for dominion and mastery had consumed him more than anything else in Eden. Adam was both proud of and worried about Cain's restless energy, as he feared his son might eventually face the same temptations he once did.

Eve, on the other hand, saw Cain's thirst for knowledge as a gift. She believed that he would grow into a person who could navigate the world with a sense of purpose and understanding. While Adam often erred on the side of caution, Eve was more open to letting their son explore and trusted his innate ability to learn from experiences in the world. Together, they tried to balance their differing perspectives, but the tension between their styles of parenting would only grow as Cain matured.

THE TENSION BETWEEN THE FAMILIAR AND THE UNKNOWN

Cain's internal conflict about staying with his parents in familiar comfort versus venturing into the unknown reflects the tension that many people feel when they step into adulthood and face daunting but necessary unknowns.

His journey centered around this theme of searching for purpose within a wider world, echoing the shared human experience of outgrowing familial expectations to claim one's own identity.

But with this new beginning came new challenges. As Cain grew, so did his emotional complexity. He had inherited curiosity from his mother, Eve, but there was a certain restlessness in him—to prove himself and stand out. Adam saw this trait in Cain from an early age, reminding him of his own time back in Eden when he had desired dominion and mastery over everything else. Cain's restless energy both pleased and troubled Adam, for he feared that his son might one day face the same temptations he had.

Eve, on the other hand, saw Cain's thirst for knowledge as a gift. She believed that he would grow into a person who could navigate the world with a sense of purpose and understanding. Adam was usually more cautious, but Eve encouraged their son to explore freely by trusting in his ability to learn from the world. Together, they tried to balance their differing perspectives, but the tension between their styles of parenting would only grow as Cain matured.

THE TENSION BETWEEN THE FAMILIAR AND THE UNKNOWN

Cain's internal conflict between staying with his parents in the safety of a familiar world and venturing into unknown territory reflects a tension many individuals experience as they grow up to adulthood and face daunting but necessary challenges.

CAIN'S CHILDHOOD AND GROWING RESTLESSNESS

As Cain grew older, his need for independence became increasingly evident. He began to question everything around him—not just the world his parents had created, but also life itself. While Adam and Eve nurtured him with love and care, Cain's inner world was often filled with confusion and a desire to understand his place in the world. A part of him felt out of place within the quiet, pastoral life his parents had built. He often wandered the fields, staring at the sky, wondering what lay beyond the boundaries of their small existence.

He began to ask questions that Adam and Eve were not always prepared to answer. "Why are we here?" Cain would ask, his voice full of the weight of his burgeoning awareness. "What is the point of all this? Why is everything so imperfect?"

Eve, ever the nurturer, would respond with patience. "We are here to learn, Cain. To understand the world and make it better. Imperfection is part of what makes us human."

But Adam, less certain of his own answers, struggled to find the right words. He was always a person of action, and though he learned much from the land, he wasn't sure how to help his son navigate these complex questions of existence.

As Cain grew older, the questions deepened. He wanted more than just answers—he wanted to experience life for himself. He wanted to test the boundaries of what he had been taught, to see if there was something more out there for him.

It was during one of these moments of deep restlessness that Cain first left the small camp they called home. He did not tell his parents where he was going. He simply set out, driven by the need to find his own path, to define himself on his own terms.

CHAPTER 18:
Cain's Exploration of the World

Meanwhile, away from his parents' land, Cain was starting his own journey into the wider world. The world beyond his childhood was new, raw, and full of potential—yet also a space in which he was haunted. He bore the burden of his actions—killing his brother Abel—as if it were a shadow that never truly left him.

Cain wandered through barren landscapes and bustling villages, crossing wide rivers and high mountains. He met many people along the way—some kind and welcoming, others cold and indifferent. In the bustling towns, he found a world full of ambition, greed, and power. He observed men and women, driven by their desires for wealth, status, and power. It was a world where survival depended not just on hard work but on cunning and, sometimes, ruthless competition.

Cain's journey was fuelled by a search for belongingness, a place where he could truly realise his identity and purpose. His story speaks to the universal struggle of finding where one fits in. Cain's departure from home underscores the push and pull between the comfort of known things and defining oneself through new experiences. His journey reflects the challenges of breaking free from the expectations of others to define one's own path.

As he travelled, Cain found himself both attracted to ambition in others and repelled by it. It reminded him of his own destructive urge—his desire to be recognised, to assert his dominance. But there was also something in these people that fascinated him. They had found ways to build communities, to create something meaningful out of the chaos of existence. And while Cain was not sure he could ever fully embrace that world, he began to see that there were other paths to be taken.

His journey became one of self-discovery. At times, he thought of returning to his parents, of finding redemption in their eyes. But each time, he was confronted by his own shame. Though simple, the world he had left behind was also a world of judgment. He dreaded their disapproval, knowing it would never undo his wrongs.

In his solitude, Cain began to face deeper truths about himself. He was not simply a murderer. He was a man shaped by his choices, by the emotions that had driven him. As he now perceived it, the world was not black and white. It was full of contradictions. It was filled with people who, like him, were trying to find their way by balancing their desires and their actions.

While Cain seeks his place in the world, Adam and Eve's journey will also evolve as they continue to learn from the land, their environment, and each other. Their ongoing search for meaning will guide them through the next phases of their lives, and they will come to understand the deeper implications of their choices.

KEY THEMES IN THIS CHAPTER

The Weight of the Past: Cain's journey is a struggle with his own past—the murder of Abel—and how it continues to shape his every step. His internal conflict is a key theme, highlighting the tension between the desire for redemption and the weight of guilt.

The Complexity of Human Nature: Through Cain's exploration of the world, we see the complexity of human nature. The world is not just a place of good and evil; it is a place where people, like Cain, must navigate their own inner struggles and try to make sense of their actions.

The Search for Identity: Cain's journey is a search for his own identity. As he encounters different people and experiences, he begins to see that his life is not defined by his past mistakes but by the choices he makes moving forward. His journey is one of self-discovery, learning to live with the complexity of who he is.

Cain will continue to encounter various cultures and people who will challenge his understanding of himself and his place in the world. This will push him toward personal growth and understanding, as well as further test his capacity for change.

REDEMPTION ACROSS RELIGIOUS TRADITIONS

The theme of redemption is a central tenet in many religious traditions, each offering unique interpretations of humanity's relationship with the divine and the journey toward reconciliation.

Christianity: In Christian theology, the narrative of the Fall is intricately tied to the promise of redemption through Jesus Christ. The concept of original sin, derived from Adam and Eve's disobedience, sets the stage for the necessity of salvation. Christians believe that Christ's sacrifice on the cross serves as the ultimate act of redemption, offering humanity a path back to a harmonious relationship with God. The New Testament echoes the hope of restoration, emphasising that through faith, believers can be renewed and reconciled to God.

Judaism: In Jewish tradition, the story of Adam and Eve also serves as a foundational narrative, but it focuses on themes of responsibility and repentance. The concept of teshubah, or returning to God, is central in Jewish thought. The actions of Adam and Eve lead to a lifelong journey of learning, moral growth, and striving for righteousness. The teachings of the Torah emphasise that, while sin carries consequences, the path to redemption lies in sincere repentance and the pursuit of justice and compassion.

Islam: In Islam, Adam and Eve are revered as the first humans, and their story emphasises both their Fall and their subsequent repentance. The Quran highlights that they were forgiven by God after acknowledging their sin. This narrative reinforces the belief in God's mercy and the possibility of redemption for all believers. The concept of returning to God through sincere faith and charitable deeds is central in Islamic teachings, illustrating that human beings are continuously on a path of growth and reconciliation.

Hinduism and Buddhism: While not focused specifically on the Eden narrative, these traditions also explore themes of fall and redemption through concepts of karma and dharma. In Hinduism, the cycle of birth, death, and rebirth (samsara) offers opportunities for growth and redemption through righteous living and the pursuit of moksha (liberation). Buddhism emphasises the potential for enlightenment and liberation from suffering through mindful living and compassion. Both traditions stress the importance of individual choices in shaping one's destiny and achieving a state of harmony with the universe.

PHILOSOPHICAL REFLECTIONS ON REDEMPTION AND GROWTH

Beyond religious contexts, philosophical reflections on redemption and growth offer valuable insights into the human experience. Thinkers across the ages have grappled with the implications of the Fall and the nature of moral choice.

Augustine: St. Augustine, a pivotal figure in Christian philosophy, viewed the Fall as an essential part of the human journey. He argued that through sin, humanity gains the awareness of its own limitations and the necessity of divine grace. Redemption, in Augustine's view, involves a transformation of the self—an inward journey toward humility and reliance on God's mercy.

Kierkegaard: Søren Kierkegaard, a nineteenth-century philosopher, emphasised the importance of individual choice and subjective experience. He believed that the journey toward redemption is deeply personal, requiring individuals to confront their despair and seek authentic faith. Kierkegaard's ideas highlight that growth often emerges from struggle and that the path to redemption is fraught with challenges.

Modern Perspectives: Contemporary philosophical discussions around redemption often focus on personal responsibility and moral development. Thinkers such as Martha Nussbaum advocate for the cultivation of empathy and compassion as pathways to personal and societal redemption. The emphasis on relational ethics reflects a broader understanding of redemption as a collective journey, where individuals strive for growth not only for themselves but for the betterment of their communities.

LESSONS FOR TODAY'S WORLD

The themes of redemption and growth found in the Eden narrative resonate powerfully in today's world, where individuals and societies face myriad challenges. The story serves as a reminder of the importance of accountability, compassion, and the potential for renewal.

Accountability: The Fall teaches us about the consequences of our actions. In a world rife with conflict and division, embracing personal responsibility and acknowledging our role in shaping our communities can pave the way for healing and reconciliation.

Compassion: The journey of Adam and Eve underscores the need for empathy in our interactions with others. Understanding that everyone is on their path of growth allows us to foster compassion, providing support to those who struggle. In a time when polarisation is prevalent, the call to love and support one another is more vital than ever.

The Quest for Meaning: The search for redemption encourages individuals to explore their beliefs and values. It invites reflection on what it means to live a meaningful life, one that prioritises growth, connection, and the pursuit of justice.

Hope in Adversity: The enduring promise of redemption reminds us that even in the darkest moments, hope is a powerful force. The narrative encourages resilience, suggesting that adversity can lead to profound growth and transformation.

EDEN'S LEGACY IN OUR LIVES

The legacy of Eden transcends time and culture, influencing art, literature, and spiritual thought. It serves as a lens through which we can understand our own experiences of loss, growth, and the quest for meaning.

Cultural Impact: The story of Adam and Eve has inspired countless works of art, literature, and music. From John Milton's *Paradise Lost* to contemporary interpretations in film and theatre, the themes of the Fall and Redemption continue to captivate the human imagination.

Personal Reflection: For many, the story prompts introspection about personal choices and moral dilemmas. It invites individuals to consider their own paths toward growth and redemption, fostering a deeper understanding of their motivations and desires.

Interconnectedness: The narrative of Eden highlights the interconnectedness of humanity's journey. The struggles faced by Adam and Eve echo throughout history, reminding us that we are all part of a larger narrative—one that encompasses the pursuit of truth, justice, and compassion.

Spiritual Exploration: Ultimately, the legacy of Eden invites individuals to explore their spiritual beliefs and the nature of their relationship with the divine. It encourages seekers to reflect on the questions of existence, morality, and the possibility of redemption in their lives.

As we wrap up this exploration of redemption, the story of Adam and Eve emerges not merely as an ancient tale but rather a profound reflection on the human experience. Themes of choice, consequence, and the quest for restoration resonate across time and culture to offer timeless lessons for our lives.

In our own journeys, we learn that redemption isn't just one event; it's an ongoing process—a constant invitation to grow and learn, seeking connection both with the divine and each other. The legacy of Eden continues to inspire us, urging us to accept our complex existence while holding on to hope for renewal and redemption.

THE ENDURING LEGACY OF EDEN: THE ECHO OF EDEN AND THE ROLE OF RELATIONSHIP

The Garden of Eden narrative captures something essential about the human condition: innocence, choice, and redemption. Through Adam and Eve, we see our deepest longings revealed, a mirror to our struggles, an intimacy with something greater than ourselves. Their journey from creation to exile reminds us that life is as much about our relationships as it is about personal growth. Eden originally was a place of divine connection and companionship/relationship in its true form.

The Garden of Eden isn't merely an origin story; it's a narrative that delves into the profound questions of human existence and continues to echo in our hearts and minds across cultures and beliefs. From its depiction of innocence and harmony to the profound journey of loss, choice, and redemption, Eden offers a timeless exploration of who we are, why we strive, and what it means to live meaningfully. In the story of Adam and Eve, we find echoes of our own lives—our longings, our struggles, our doubts, and our ceaseless search for connection.

The Eden story reminds us of the beauty and fragility of innocence and the inevitability of growth. In the blissful state of paradise, Adam and Eve were not acquainted with shame or fear, only an intimate connection with each other, nature, and their Maker. Yet, as their fateful choice led them from innocence to awareness, it symbolised the journey each of us faces: the realisation of our own agency, the awareness of our flaws, and the acceptance of our responsibility in shaping our lives and relationships.

The central theme of choice and consequence runs deep in the Eden narrative. Adam and Eve's decision to eat the forbidden fruit reveals the complexity of human freedom. By choosing knowledge, they entered a morally complex world where their actions have consequences—and in that struggle, growth often occurs. Their story serves as a reminder that the choices we make, however challenging, shape our character and destiny. It also underscores the idea that growth and wisdom come not from avoiding mistakes but from facing them with courage and humility.

The biblical exile from Eden—the painful separation from paradise—is analogous to a universal human experience. We each face moments of exile and loss, times when we are forced to navigate the wilderness of uncertainty, hardship, and doubt. Yet, like Adam and Eve, we also carry within us the capacity for resilience, adaptation, and the pursuit of purpose. Outside of Eden, we are challenged to forge meaningful connections, cultivate compassion, and find fulfilment in the richness of life's journey.

What would Eden have been without Eve? This question highlights an important aspect of the human story: our need for connection and how relationships shape our quest for meaning. Had Adam been alone in Eden, the garden would have been devoid of one of its most essential elements—the experience of companionship and shared purpose. God's creation of Eve is a testament to this truth that "It is not good for man to be alone," woven into the fabric of human experience. The richness of Eden was not in its physical beauty alone, but in the relational dynamic it held, a dynamic made possible through the presence of both Adam and Eve.

Without Eve, life in Eden would have been limited in ways that go beyond the physical. Adam's relationship with God would have remained central. However, without a fellow human to share his experiences, his capacity for self-understanding, empathy, and growth would have been incomplete. Eve's presence brought the possibility of mutual love, understanding, and collaboration, allowing Adam to see himself reflected in another being and fostering a fuller sense of purpose.

Moreover, Eve's presence introduced the potential for choice and change that ultimately led to the development of human consciousness. Taking the forbidden fruit was not a mere act of individual choice, but rather a shared journey that led them to face consequences from seeking knowledge and independence. Together, they represent humanity's collective experience— the path of growth, fallibility, and the quest for redemption. This journey highlights that life, even in paradise, is incomplete without relationships, without shared experiences and the challenges that come with them.

Eve's presence in Eden is a necessity not only for companionship but also to enable the continuation of humanity. Without Eve, Adam would have remained alone, unable to fulfil one of the foundational purposes of human existence: to "be fruitful and multiply." This mandate, given by God in the Genesis story, emphasises that creation is meant to be dynamic, expansive, and self-perpetuating. Without Eve, Adam's life in the Garden would have been static, limiting the human experience to a solitary existence without growth or legacy.

Eve's creation allowed for the possibility of a future human lineage—a generation that would continue to carry forward the story of humanity. The relationship between Adam and Eve symbolises more than just companionship; it is a partnership through which humanity could flourish. Without her, there would be no children, no families, and no societies. Humanity's diversity, richness, and complexity all stem from that initial union, making Eve essential to the story of human origin. Her presence was necessary to fulfil the biological and spiritual roles that would lead to the continuation of the human story.

Furthermore, Eve's role also highlights the importance of shared responsibility and mutual growth. While Adam alone could tend the Garden and commune with God, he could not experience the relational dynamics of love, trust, and sacrifice that arise within family and community. Eve brought the possibility of new relationships and expanded the scope of human experience beyond the individual. Through her, Adam could learn to nurture, protect, and grow with another being, laying the groundwork for a more complex, interconnected humanity.

Without Eve, Adam's role in the Garden would have remained limited, as he would never experience the personal growth and challenges that come with relationships, parenthood, and community. In this sense, Eve's presence is the gateway to a fuller, richer human experience. Through their union and the generations that followed, the human story unfolds in its myriad forms—each life an extension of that first connection. Eve's role, then, is foundational not only as a companion but as the mother of humanity, symbolising the continuity, diversity, and depth that define the human journey.

Thus, Eve is not merely Adam's partner; she is humanity's beginning. Without her, the Garden would have been the end of the story, with no descendants to learn, grow, and seek meaning. Her role exemplifies the power of relationships to transcend the individual, allowing life to extend beyond oneself and connecting each generation to the next. Through her, humanity finds its purpose, potential, and future—fulfilling the Garden's promise to grow, flourish, and embrace the fullness of life.

The Eden story thus speaks to the human need for companionship and the ways in which relationships shape us. It reflects our natural inclination to seek understanding and support from others and illustrates that true fulfilment arises not from isolation, but from the interconnectedness of our lives. The presence of Eve not only completed the picture of paradise but also set in motion the journey that led to the discovery of the human spirit's strength and resilience.

As we reflect on Eden and its legacy, we are reminded of the importance of relationships in our own lives. Like Adam, we are shaped by our connections, our bonds with others, and the choices we make within those relationships. The journey of Adam and Eve is a testament to the richness and complexity that companionship brings, even when it leads to challenge and growth.

In the echo of Eden, may we remember that paradise is not just a place, but an experience shared. It is in our relationships—with each other and with the divine—that we find the essence of life. The story of Adam and Eve is a reminder that we are not meant to walk alone. Through our connections, we experience the beauty, challenge, and profound meaning that Eden symbolises—a paradise that lives on in the relationships that define us and the enduring hope for redemption.

The Eden story bears witness to humanity's persistent hope for redemption and reconciliation. Across religious, philosophical, and cultural traditions, the theme of redemption offers a vision of restoration, a promise that even in a world marked by struggle and separation, we can find a path toward healing and wholeness. Whether through faith, relationships, or the pursuit of wisdom, our quest for redemption reflects our deepest longing to restore what was lost, to bridge the gap between ourselves and the divine, and to find peace within ourselves.

As we leave Eden behind, we are reminded that the journey of humanity mirrors the journey of Adam and Eve. Each of us carries the imprint of paradise—a desire for harmony, beauty, and connection—and each of us faces the reality of choices, challenges, and growth. Reflecting on the Eden story invites us to ponder our choices, value systems, and sources of inspiration. Thus, we become part of a larger—timeless—journey: one which leads to self-discovery, purpose, and the enduring quest for meaning.

In Eden's echo, may we find the courage to face our choices, the resilience to overcome our struggles, and the wisdom to seek redemption in all that we do. May we honour the legacy of Eden not as a distant myth, but as a living story—a reminder that in every choice, every act of compassion, and every step toward growth, we carry a piece of paradise within us.

What happened to the Garden of Eden after Adam and Eve were expelled is another intriguing mystery in the Genesis story. While the Bible does not go into details about Eden's fate, various biblical and extra-biblical sources provide different interpretations on what might have happened to it or its symbolic meaning.

THE GARDEN AFTER THE EXIT OF ADAM AND EVE

1.   The Immediate Aftermath of the Expulsion

In Genesis 3:23–24, God expelled Adam and Eve from the garden after their disobedience so that they could "work the ground from which [Adam] was taken." Their exile marks the end of their access to the abundant, untroubled life they had enjoyed in Eden. To prevent any future attempt at re-entry and retrieval of immortality from the Tree of Life, God stations cherubim (angelic guardians) and a "flaming sword" at the east of the garden. This barrier reinforces the finality of their separation from Eden and the unbridgeable divide between the sacred garden and the outside world.

2.   The Garden as a Lost Paradise

The guarded entry implies that Eden might still exist, though now hidden or beyond human reach. This interpretation has led to centuries of speculation about Eden's physical location, with various theories proposing it might be found somewhere on Earth or hidden in a supernatural realm. Many ancient traditions suggest Eden was indeed real but sacred; humans cannot re-enter owing to their fallen state.

Over time, the idea of Eden transformed into a vision of paradise that awaits in the afterlife for the righteous. In this way, Eden becomes less a physical location and more an archetype of divine perfection, peace, and harmony, echoing the conditions of a restored relationship with God. The cherubim and the flaming sword then symbolise the separation not only from a place but from a state of spiritual harmony with God and nature.

3.   Speculations on Eden's Physical Location and Fate

Various religious and historical sources attempt to locate Eden geographically. Some early Jewish, Christian, and Islamic scholars proposed that Eden could be found somewhere in Mesopotamia, near the Tigris and Euphrates rivers (which are named in Genesis 2). Others placed it at the top of a sacred mountain, a symbol of divine presence. However, owing to a lack of definitive evidence, the exact location remains speculative.

Some interpretations suggest that the physical garden was destroyed or faded away over time. This view sees Eden as a sacred space that was removed from Earth, taken up into the heavens, hidden, or even eradicated as the world became increasingly corrupt after humanity's Fall. The flood narrative in Genesis 6–9, in which God floods the earth in response to widespread human sin, has sometimes been seen as a final erasure of any remnants of Eden's purity from the physical world.

4.   Eden as a Symbolic or Spiritual Realm

Many religious traditions see Eden as a spiritual realm, not a physical place on Earth. In this interpretation, Eden exists as a divine archetype—a perfect state of being that is beyond human reach in a fallen world. In Christian theology, Eden is often regarded as a foreshadowing of heaven, a place of eternal peace, unity with God, and freedom from suffering.

This symbolic understanding of Eden underscores its role in humanity's spiritual journey. Rather than a literal place that could be rediscovered, Eden represents the ideal relationship between God and humanity, which was lost but can potentially be restored. The garden thus becomes an aspirational vision of paradise, one that is accessible only through spiritual reconciliation and, ultimately, through redemption in the afterlife.

5.   The Garden in Religious Tradition and Eschatology

In some Jewish and Christian eschatological teachings, Eden will be restored at the end of time as part of the new creation. In Revelation 22, the vision of the new heaven and new earth includes imagery reminiscent of Eden, particularly the Tree of Life, which appears along the river in the New Jerusalem. This vision suggests that Eden, or the state it represents, will be restored in the future, signifying ultimate reconciliation of God with creation.

This theme of restoration appears in other religious texts as well. For instance, in Islam, Eden (known as "Jannah") is seen as the original paradise and the future dwelling place of the righteous. In Islamic teachings, Eden awaits the faithful in the afterlife, a place of reward that echoes the perfection and beauty of the original Garden.

6.   Eden's Legacy in Cultural and Literary Traditions

The story of Eden has inspired countless interpretations in literature, art, and philosophy. From John Milton's *Paradise Lost*, which explores themes of innocence, loss, and redemption, to more recent reflections on humanity's disconnection from nature, Eden is often invoked as a symbol of a lost world or a pure state that humanity continually yearns to recover.

In modern ecological thought, Eden is sometimes viewed as a metaphor for an unspoiled earth, a vision of balance and sustainability that humans are called to respect and protect. This perspective reinterprets the garden as an ideal of ecological stewardship, suggesting that while we may never physically return to Eden, we can work toward creating a balanced and harmonious relationship with the natural world.

CONCLUSION: EDEN AS BOTH A LOST PLACE AND A CONTINUING IDEAL

After Adam and Eve's expulsion, the Garden of Eden takes on a mysterious and complex role in biblical narrative—and beyond. Whether seen as a hidden physical place, spiritual ideal, or a lost paradise to be restored someday, Eden symbolises humanity's longing for wholeness, peace, and unity with the divine and nature. Its fate remains a mystery, inviting reflection on themes of separation, loss, and the hope for eventual reconciliation—a reminder of a harmony that humanity once experienced and continues to seek.

CHAPTER 19:
Modern Relevance of Eden
Psychological Interpretations

In Jungian psychology, the story of Eden can be interpreted as a symbolic journey from the unconscious unity of existence to the birth of individual ego consciousness. Here is a detailed explanation of how this interpretation unfolds:

1. **Eden as the Unconscious:**

Unity and Wholeness: Eden stands for the initial stage of wholeness in the unconscious, under Jungian interpretation. Adam and Eve live in a harmonious, unselfconscious state where they feel complete, connected with God and nature, reflecting the pre-ego, undifferentiated unconscious mind. This ties into Jung's idea of the collective unconscious, a shared psychic realm filled with archetypes and primordial images that represent our original state.

Innocence and Lack of Duality: In the unconscious, opposites like good and evil, light and dark, are not yet separated. This is mirrored in Adam and Eve's innocence and unity within Eden, where they have no awareness of dual concepts such as morality or shame. They live without self-consciousness, like the child's psyche before developing a clear sense of individual self.

2. **The Fruit of Knowledge as the Call to Consciousness:**

The Serpent as a Catalyst for Awareness: The serpent in Jungian thought can represent the pull toward self-knowledge and individualism. The serpent tempts Eve to eat the fruit, acting as a force that draws human consciousness away from the unconscious and encourages it to discover knowledge, duality, and the self. This action causes Adam and Eve to awaken to a sense of "I" and "Other."

Awakening of Duality and the Birth of Moral Awareness: By eating the fruit of knowledge, Adam and Eve become aware of dualities such as good and evil, life and death, nakedness and shame. This is a pivotal moment in Jungian psychology, as it signifies the birth of ego consciousness—the formation of an identity that sees itself as separate from the larger whole.

3.   Expulsion as the Emergence of Ego Consciousness:

Leaving the Garden as a Rite of Passage: Being cast out of Eden signifies moving from unconscious wholeness to conscious separation. This aligns with the development of the ego, the part of the mind that separates the individual self from the collective unconscious. In Jungian terms, this is necessary for psychological growth, as it leads to the development of self-awareness and moral autonomy.

The "Fall" as the Birth of Selfhood: In Jung's perspective, the so-called "Fall" from Eden is not inherently negative but rather an essential step in the individuation process. Leaving Eden's safety and unity is when Adam and Eve begin to journey toward becoming whole, individuated selves. Though this entails pain and loss, through the separation they gain potential for true self-knowledge and wisdom.

Conscious Struggle as a Path to Wholeness: Outside Eden, Adam and Eve face pain, labour, and mortality, representing the difficulties of conscious life. However, this path is also the way toward individuation, a key Jungian concept that involves integrating the conscious ego with the deeper aspects of the unconscious, ultimately leading to a sense of wholeness or "self" that transcends mere ego.

4.   **Jung's Idea of Reuniting with the Unconscious:**

Individuation and the Goal of Reconciliation: Jung believed that the goal of psychological development is to reconcile the ego with the unconscious, integrating them into a unified self. The story of Eden, then, can be seen as a mythic journey that every person undergoes: first, a Fall into separateness and self-awareness, then, through individuation, a gradual reintegration of the ego and unconscious.

The Garden as an Archetype of Paradise: Eden represents the archetypal memory of a paradise state, a longing that resides in each person's unconscious. In Jungian psychology, this longing for the lost "garden" manifests in dreams, myths, and spiritual pursuits, symbolising a desire to regain the unity and wholeness of the original unconscious state, but now with the added depth of conscious awareness.

5.   **Symbolic Integration of Good and Evil:**

Duality as a Necessary Part of Consciousness: The knowledge of good and evil gained through the fruit represents the ego's need to confront and integrate opposing forces within the psyche. According to Jung, true psychological wholeness—the self—involves both light and shadow. The expulsion, then, is the beginning of this lifelong task of integrating dualities, and only through confronting these can individuals reach higher consciousness and self-realisation.

In Eden, Adam and Eve were sheltered from hardship. Outside, they learn that growth often comes through struggle, not comfort. Their new life shows that perfection can be limiting, while imperfection allows for transformation, progress, and the pursuit of meaning. Outside Eden, Eve's role as the mother of humanity gains prominence. She embodies the continuity of life, symbolising resilience, fertility, and the hope that future generations will find ways to thrive. Her title as the "Mother of All Living" reflects the concept of life persevering despite hardship and loss.

The loss of Eden leaves Adam and Eve yearning for an idealised past, but it also opens a path toward a richer, more complex existence. Humanity must learn to create its own "paradise" through hard work, creativity, and moral growth, rather than relying on an ideal state provided by another. This represents the potential for human agency in creating a better future.

In a sense, the expulsion from Eden marks the beginning of the human story—a journey marked by trial, growth, discovery, and the continuous search for meaning. Through Adam and Eve's story, humanity's journey unfolds as one filled with both beauty and struggle, forging a path forward with courage and hope.

IN SUMMARY

Life outside Eden symbolises the complexities of human existence. While Eden represents an idealised innocence, the world outside it reflects the full scope of human experience: responsibility, moral awareness, hard work, relationships, and a search for spiritual connection. Adam and Eve's journey suggests that human life, with all its challenges and imperfections, is a valuable process of growth, transformation, and the quest for meaning. Rather than an end, their expulsion marks the beginning of humanity's journey, one in which individuals must navigate the realities of life, striving to create their own sense of purpose and beauty in a world of both struggle and possibility.

In Jungian psychology, Eden is more than a paradise lost; it symbolises the unconscious mind in a state of primal unity. The expulsion represents the awakening of ego consciousness—a necessary development that enables growth, self-awareness, and the potential for individuation and spiritual maturity. Through this symbolic journey, humanity progresses from innocence to a more profound wisdom that encompasses both knowledge of the self and a deepened, conscious connection to the greater whole.

ENVIRONMENTAL SYMBOLISM

The story of Eden can be seen as an ecological parable that symbolises humanity's relationship with nature, and it warns of the consequences associated with overstepping natural boundaries and exploiting the environment.

1.   **Eden as an Ideal State of Harmony with Nature:**

Paradise as Ecological Balance: Eden is shown as a pure, self-sustaining ecosystem where all beings live in harmony. Adam and Eve inhabit this garden to "tend and keep it," not engage in reckless dominance or consumption. This represents an ideal ecological balance, where humans are stewards and guardians—not conquerors or exploiters.

The loss of Eden fills Adam and Eve with a longing for a golden age, yet it also offers an opportunity to live a richer and fuller life. Humans should make their own "paradise" by working hard, being creative, and developing virtues—rather than relying on an external, ideal state. This shows that human agency can positively affect the future.

Living Within Limits: In Eden, Adam and Eve live without taking more than is offered. They can eat from all trees but one, portraying the idea of respectful restraint amidst abundance. This limit serves as a metaphor for respecting natural boundaries, acknowledging that some parts of nature should remain untouched to maintain ecological balance.

In Eden, Adam and Eve were sheltered from hardship. Outside, they learn that growth often comes through struggle, not comfort. Their new life indicates that perfection can be stifling; imperfection allows for transformation and progress toward finding meaning.

2.   **The Forbidden Fruit as a Symbol of Greed and Overreach:**

The forbidden fruit symbolises humanity's desire to extract more from nature than it is entitled to. By eating from the Tree of Knowledge, Adam and Eve go beyond their role as caretakers—driven by a desire to have power or knowledge not meant for them. This act mirrors humanity's tendency to exploit resources driven by greed or arrogance, reflected in a destructive impulse to exceed natural limits.

Eating the fruit represents humanity's urge to control and manipulate nature for personal gain, rather than maintaining a humble relationship with it. In this sense, the fruit symbolises acts like deforestation, pollution, or unsustainable resource extraction—all driven by an unchecked desire to have more even at the cost of disrupting natural balance.

3.   Expulsion as a Loss of Connection with Nature:

Being expelled from Eden, Adam and Eve are removed from the natural abundance and harmony of the garden. This serves as a metaphor for humanity's gradual alienation from nature. Once outside of Eden, they must work hard to produce food and suffer in their relationship with the land—symbolising a fractured connection with nature.

God's punishment: Adam will have to labour "by the sweat of his brow" in tilling the earth; this foreshadows the ecological consequences of exploitation. This laborious struggle with the land symbolises the increased difficulty of survival when natural resources are strained or depleted. Just as humans today face the environmental consequences of deforestation, pollution, and climate change, Adam's struggle with the land reflects the challenge of living in a degraded world.

4.   Environmental Symbolism of the Serpent:

In ecological terms, the serpent can be seen as representing forces that encourage human beings to misuse or disrupt nature. The serpent's promise that Adam and Eve will "be like God" echoes the idea that humans can achieve power and control over nature. By listening to this voice, they begin believing that it is possible to transcend natural limits. This parallels the modern drive—to dominate and reshape the environment without regard for balance or sustainability.

5.   Eden as a Prototype of Earth's Ecosystem:

Just as Eden is a unique environment filled with diverse flora and fauna, our planet's ecosystems are delicately balanced networks of life. Eden symbolises Earth in its natural, untouched form prior to human intervention. The story implies that when humans act out of selfishness or shortsightedness, they risk turning their "paradise" into a place of struggle and scarcity.

By disrupting the harmonious order of Eden, Adam and Eve lose access to its abundant resources. Similarly, when humans disrupt ecosystems through pollution, habitat destruction, and climate change, they risk the health and stability of these environments. Eden, in this sense, serves as a reminder of the beauty and richness that can exist when humans respect natural limits, as well as the losses that come when these limits are ignored.

6. The Need for Environmental Stewardship:

The biblical charge given to Adam and Eve to tend the garden reflects the concept of environmental stewardship—caring for the Earth as guardians rather than exploiters. In ecological terms, the story of Eden suggests that humanity's role is to protect and preserve the natural world, maintaining balance rather than exploiting it for short-term gains.

When Adam and Eve disregard this role, they bring disorder and suffering upon themselves, suggesting that when humans act out of greed and disrespect for nature, they harm themselves. This is a profound ecological message that underscores the interconnectedness of human and environmental well-being.

7. The Fall as an Ecological Warning:

On a symbolic level, the expulsion from Eden can be seen as a warning that if humanity ignores natural order and pursues knowledge and power without wisdom, it risks destroying the paradise in which it lives. Humanity's Fall from grace in Eden serves as a powerful allegory for the ecological consequences of environmental exploitation. Once lost, harmony with nature may be difficult—if not impossible—to fully restore.

Eden's story suggests that while humans have a unique capacity for knowledge and creativity, this must be balanced by restraint, respect for nature, and acknowledgment of ecological limits. If humanity continues to live unsustainably, the "Fall" from nature's grace may come with dire consequences. This includes, but is not limited to, environmental degradation and loss of biodiversity.

IN SUMMARY

When viewed through an ecological lens, the story of Eden can be understood as a parable that warns against environmental exploitation. Eden represents a world of abundance, balance, and interdependence—a paradise in which humanity lives as a caretaker rather than a ruler. By overreaching and consuming the forbidden fruit, Adam and Eve disrupt this harmony and are cast out, symbolising humanity's loss of its natural paradise and foretelling the consequences of environmental disregard. This interpretation suggests that true paradise is found when humanity respects the earth and lives in balance with nature, and it warns of the hardships that arise when we forget this essential relationship.

FEMINIST REINTERPRETATIONS

Feminist reinterpretations of the Eden narrative have provided a fresh perspective on Eve's role, questioning traditional readings that cast her as the source of sin and downfall. Instead of blaming Eve, modern feminist scholars explore her as a complex figure who embodies autonomy, curiosity, and agency. These reinterpretations seek to dismantle patriarchal frameworks that have historically justified women's subordination by portraying Eve—and by extension, all women—as inherently flawed, weak, or dangerous.

Here are some key insights and contributions from feminist scholarship on Eve:

1. **Reclaiming Eve's Curiosity and Autonomy**

Traditional interpretations often view Eve's curiosity as a flaw—an impulsive sin that brings suffering to humanity. Feminist scholars argue that this interpretation reflects a patriarchal bias that discourages female inquiry, autonomy, and self-assertion. Eve's decision to eat the fruit can instead be seen as an exercise of intellectual curiosity and desire for knowledge, qualities that are often praised in men but criticised in women.

Eve's decision to eat the fruit shows her autonomy and agency, rejecting her passivity as a companion. Some feminist readings celebrate Eve's decision as a bold act of self-determination, portraying her as a figure who refuses to accept ignorance and submission. Her actions show an assertion of free will, implying that Eve is one of the earliest feminist figures who make independent choices despite their consequences.

2. The "Original Sin" as a Misinterpretation of Female Nature

Traditional Christian interpretations have often placed the blame for the "Fall" squarely on Eve, viewing her as the source of original sin and, by extension, female inferiority. Feminist scholars like Phyllis Trible argue that these interpretations are culturally biased, reflecting the historical marginalisation of women rather than an objective reading of the text. Trible contends that Eve's story has been misused to justify misogyny and female subjugation, citing examples in which the text itself is not explicitly vilifying her in such ways as later patriarchal interpretations have done.

Scholars like Tikva Frymer-Kensky view Eve as a fully human, multidimensional character who deserves empathy rather than blame. Frymer-Kensky argues that Eve's "Fall" reflects human vulnerability rather than any inherent flaw in women. This interpretation sees Eve as representing universal human experience with temptation, curiosity, and moral choices—a figure to be empathised with rather than seen as guilty or shameful.

3. Eve's Role as the First Seeker of Knowledge

Feminist scholars such as Carol Meyers suggest that Eve's quest for knowledge symbolises a positive, even admirable, human trait—the pursuit of understanding. Meyers argues that Eve should be seen as the first seeker of wisdom, who breaks away from an imposed ignorance. In this interpretation, Eve is not a passive transgressor but an active participant in humanity's journey toward consciousness, embodying the courage and strength to explore the unknown.

Some feminists see Eve's decision to eat the fruit as a bold step into intellectual freedom. By choosing knowledge over obedience, she can be seen as the first philosopher, a figure who dares to question and explore rather than accept authority blindly. In this sense, Eve's "sin" is her desire for wisdom—a quality that feminist scholars argue should be celebrated rather than condemned.

4. Challenging the Narrative of Female Weakness and Passivity

Traditional readings have often depicted Eve as gullible and easily deceived by the serpent, reinforcing stereotypes about female susceptibility to temptation. Feminist theologians like Rosemary Radford Ruether challenge this view, suggesting that it reflects a cultural bias that paints women as intellectually inferior to men. Ruether argues that Eve's interaction with the serpent shows her as an active participant in the decision, willing to question and engage rather than passively follow.

Rather than seeing Eve as a mere sidekick or subservient figure, feminist interpretations view her as Adam's equal in the narrative. Eve's actions, while traditionally condemned, are crucial to the development of human consciousness and moral awareness. She is portrayed as a co-creator in humanity's journey—representing partnership rather than subordination.

5. Redefining the Nature of "The Fall"

Some feminist scholars reframe the Fall as a necessary step in humanity's journey from innocence to self-awareness. By eating the fruit, Eve opens the door to human consciousness, moral knowledge, and individuality, paving the way for human development and progress. Feminist theologians like Elaine Pagels argue that this reinterpretation casts the Fall as a transformation, a symbolic "birth" of human awareness, rather than a downfall. From this perspective, Eve should not be seen as a source of shame but honoured as the mother of human knowledge.

For feminists, Eve's story is a universal tale about the cost of human freedom and self-awareness. Rather than focusing on Eve's gender, feminist scholars see the narrative as a story about choices and consequences that define human experience—with Eve symbolising courage and resilience instead of being made into a scapegoat.

6.   Eve as a Feminist Icon

Many feminist scholars argue that traditional interpretations of Eve's story have served to justify patriarchal power structures by portraying women as inherently flawed. Feminists trying to reclaim Eve's story wish to turn her into an icon of female autonomy and strength. Eve is no longer seen as a passive figure punished for her curiosity but as an individual who challenges boundaries and pursues knowledge, embodying feminist ideals of independence and self-determination.

For some feminists, Eve's defiance represents a refusal to accept the constraints placed upon her. By aligning her with figures of resistance, this view challenges the notion that obedience is ideal. Eve's decision to eat the fruit symbolises her rejection of imposed limitations and her willingness to take risks and exercise agency—making her a role model for women's empowerment.

NOTABLE FEMINIST SCHOLARS AND THEIR CONTRIBUTIONS

Phyllis Trible: In her work *God and the Rhetoric of Sexuality*, Trible challenges traditional interpretations that cast Eve as the villain of the Genesis story, arguing that Eve's story has been misused to reinforce female inferiority.

Rosemary Radford Ruether: A pioneer of feminist theology, Ruether argues against readings that portray Eve as gullible or weaker, instead interpreting her actions as an expression of agency and independence.

Elaine Pagels: In *Adam, Eve, and the Serpent*, Pagels explores how early Christian interpretations of Eve have shaped negative views of women, and she suggests that the Fall can be read as a positive symbol of human freedom and self-awareness.

Carol Meyers: Meyers, in her studies on ancient Israelite women, interprets Eve as a complex, empowered figure who represents the strength and resilience of women rather than weakness.

Modern feminist reinterpretations of the Eden narrative reject the view that Eve's actions justify female subordination. Instead, they see her as a symbol of courage, autonomy, and intellectual curiosity, transforming her from a figure of blame into a proto-feminist icon. By reclaiming Eve's story, feminist scholars challenge patriarchal readings that have historically marginalised women, offering a perspective that celebrates Eve's complexity and strength, and ultimately portraying her as a model for female empowerment and resilience.

THE JOURNEY FROM INNOCENCE TO WISDOM

The story of Adam and Eve, when viewed through a modern perspective, conveys the universal progression from innocence to self-awareness and dependence to self-reliance. In Eden, they lived harmoniously without fear or insecurity. However, choosing to eat the fruit was a watershed moment—leaving behind paradise and gaining a life of meaning and growth. The story reveals that innocence, while comforting, is not a complete human experience. Through knowledge and self-awareness, Adam and Eve discover early on that living includes both joy and sorrow—and this embrace is what makes life uniquely beautiful.

This journey mirrors the human experience of maturation. As we grow, decisions will bring complexity into our lives. Like Adam and Eve, we find that life's richness comes not from avoiding difficulty but from engaging with it, learning from each struggle, and becoming stronger, wiser, and more compassionate. Their story then reflects our journey from innocence to wisdom.

The knowledge of good and evil that Adam and Eve acquire symbolises the acceptance of duality within themselves and within the world. In Eden, they only knew harmony, but through their choice, they became aware of life's complexities—there is both light and shadow. This knowledge was not a punishment but an invitation to see the world in its entirety. They came to understand that joy and sorrow, hope and fear, are intertwined.

For modern readers, this aspect of their story offers a reminder to embrace life's full spectrum. It suggests that true wisdom is not about achieving perpetual happiness but about accepting life's challenges and finding meaning in all its facets. Adam and Eve show us that maturity comes from recognising our capacity for both light and shadow, and from choosing to act with compassion, love, and integrity in a world that is beautifully imperfect.

One of the most profound lessons from Adam and Eve's story is the responsibility that comes with knowledge and freedom. When they choose to eat the fruit, they are choosing a life of agency—one in which their actions matter and they must face the consequences of their decisions. They learn that with knowledge comes the responsibility to live thoughtfully, with an awareness of how their actions shape not only their lives but the lives of others.

In their journey beyond Eden, Adam and Eve created a legacy of resilience, compassion, and community. They build a life for their children, imparting the values they discovered through their own struggles. Their legacy is a reminder that the choices we make reverberate through time, influencing the lives of those who come after us. It challenges us to live with purpose and to consider the impact we have on others, knowing that our actions create the foundation for future generations.

Throughout their journey, love is the force that sustains Adam and Eve. It anchors them, comforts them in uncertainty and gives strength to their bond. In Eden, their love was simple and harmonious; beyond Eden, it becomes a resilient partnership, one that deepens as they face hardship together. They learn that true love is not about ease but about mutual respect, understanding, and the willingness to grow together.

Their story speaks to the enduring power of human connection. It reminds us that love, in its truest form, is a choice we make each day—a choice to support, uplift, and cherish one another, even when life is challenging. Adam and Eve's love becomes a model for relationships rooted not just in romance but also in respect, trust, and shared purpose. In a modern world often marked by individualism, their story offers a timeless reminder of the beauty and strength found in genuine connection.

For centuries, the story of Adam and Eve was interpreted as a tale of punishment and loss. But through a modern lens, their story is reclaimed as one of growth, transformation, and courage. They are not figures to be blamed or pitied; they are heroes of a journey that reveals the fullness of human experience. By choosing knowledge over innocence, they choose to embrace life in all its complexity.

This reinterpretation invites us to see Adam and Eve not as symbols of failure, but as pioneers of a journey that each of us undertakes. They become symbols of resilience, wisdom, and the enduring power of love. In reimagining their story, we find that it resonates with our own experiences and aspirations, offering timeless insights into what it means to be human.

Ultimately, Adam and Eve's journey is a story of hope and renewal. They leave Eden, but they create a new world of their own—a world defined not by loss but by growth, not by punishment but by purpose. Their story reminds us that even when we face the unknown, even when we feel vulnerable or uncertain, we have the capacity to create beauty and meaning.

In this twenty-first-century retelling, Adam and Eve are no longer simply figures from a distant past; they are companions on our journey, showing us that life's challenges are opportunities for transformation. They remind us that we are all, in some way, stepping into the unknown, forging a path with courage, and leaving a legacy that reflects our values and our love.

In their new life beyond Eden, Adam and Eve's bond deepens, yet they feel a longing to share their love and struggles with others—to build a family and create a legacy. This desire to nurture life reflects their transformation from caretakers of Eden to creators of a new world, where they can impart the values and wisdom they have gained. A shared vision of family brings them joy and hope, offering an opportunity to shape a future that reflects their journey and growth.

The idea of children brings new energy to their lives, giving purpose to their labour and strengthening their bond. They dream of a community that will extend beyond themselves, a lineage that will carry forward the lessons they have learned about resilience, compassion, and the beauty of human connection.

THE GIFT AND CHALLENGE OF PARENTHOOD

When their first child arrives, Adam and Eve are filled with awe and gratitude. They see in their baby a reflection of their love, a life anew who contains both. Parenthood, however, brings its own set of challenges. They must learn how to care for another being, how to nurture, teach, and guide without the assurance of Eden's protections. They realise that their responsibility now extends beyond each other; they are shaping the foundation of their family, creating a legacy that will endure.

They find that parenthood deepens their understanding of both love and sacrifice. Every day brings new demands and joys, as they balance their own needs with the needs of their child. Parenthood requires patience, resilience, and an acceptance of life's unpredictability. Through their child, they experience the vulnerability of love, knowing that the well-being of another is now bound to their own.

PASSING DOWN LESSONS OF RESILIENCE AND COMPASSION

As their family grows, Adam and Eve recount tales of Eden to their children, sharing both its beauty and what challenges they faced on their journey. They truly talk about paradise, but also about their decision choosing knowledge instead of innocence. They instruct their children on the importance of curiosity, self-awareness, and bravery in facing life's uncertainties.

These tales enable their children to see that life is beautiful not only in its joys, but also in challenges. Adam and Eve teach them the importance of resilience, showing that hardship is not a punishment but a teacher, a way to discover strength and wisdom. Through their struggles, they learned compassion and kindness—and pass down these values, knowing that their children will need them as they face challenges of their own.

Their children start to view their parents not just as authority figures, but role models—people who have lived life fully and faced hardship with grace as well as gratitude. Adam and Eve's legacy is one of strength and empathy, a foundation that allows the family to keep their values alive.

BUILDING A COMMUNITY

Over time, as their children grow, Adam and Eve's family begins to take on the shape of a small community. Each person plays an integral role in their shared life, and every contribution matters. Adam and Eve beam with pride as their children learn to work together, respect each other, and appreciate one another's strengths. This community becomes a testament to their shared efforts, a living expression of the values they have worked to instil.

Their family becomes more than a source of comfort; it is a partnership rooted in a shared purpose. Together, they learn the importance of teamwork, respect, and the balance between individual freedom and collective responsibility. Adam and Eve see in their family the beginnings of a society—one based on mutual support, where each member is valued and love and resilience are central to their way of life.

THE CYCLE OF LEGACY

As Adam and Eve grow older, they begin to see the fruit of their efforts reflected in their children and the community they have built. They watch as their children pass down the values they have learned, continuing the legacy of resilience, compassion, and gratitude. Through the stories of Eden and the wisdom passed down from Adam and Eve, their descendants become caretakers.

This cycle of legacy brings a sense of peace and fulfilment to Adam and Eve. They see that their lives were not only about surviving beyond Eden but about shaping a foundation for generations to come. Their legacy is more than just a memory of paradise; it becomes part of the lives and stories told by those who follow—a heritage built on love, growth, and courage that was able to embrace the fullness of human experience.

CHAPTER 20:
A Final Reflection

As Adam and Eve reflect on their lives, they realize that it was not their Fall from Eden, but the choices they made thereafter, that defined them. They chose to seek understanding, to embrace the unknown, and to build a life founded on love and resilience. This journey of transformation and renewal has been marked by both joy and hardship—and it continues.

They see this continued journey in their family and community, as a new generation will carry forward the lessons of their lives. Adam and Eve feel profoundly at peace, knowing they lived fully, loved deeply, and have left a legacy that will endure.

Their story is now not one of innocence lost, but of life fully embraced—defined by the power and complexity of love and the courage to face uncertainty. As they look at their family, they understand that their journey was worthwhile. They became creators of a new world—a world not built on innocence, but on the ties that bind us and the enduring power of love.

The Bible specifically names three of Adam and Eve's children: Cain, Abel, and Seth; but it implies that they had many more children. Genesis 5:4 states, "After Seth was born, Adam lived 800 years and had other sons and daughters." Although Cain, Abel, and Seth are the only children named in the biblical text, many religious and historical traditions suggest that Adam and Eve may have had a large family, potentially giving rise to the early human community.

The idea that the serpent taught Adam to be romantically attracted to Eve is not found in the Genesis account of the Bible. Nevertheless, as a creative or interpretative exploration, it can be seen as symbolic to examine how humanity became aware of desire and intimacy—and all the complexities of love that led to the birth of Cain, then Abel. In this interpretation, the serpent acts not just as a tempter but as an instigator of awareness, awakening Adam to romantic attraction and deepening the bond between him and Eve.

1.   The Serpent as a Catalyst of Awareness

In the Garden of Eden, Adam and Eve are portrayed as living in innocence—not knowing their own nakedness or being aware of the complexities of human emotions, including romantic and sexual attraction.

The serpent, as a symbol of cunning and knowledge, could be reimagined as the one who illuminates Adam's understanding of Eve, encouraging him to recognize her beauty, personality, and significance beyond companionship.

2.   Romantic Attraction as a Natural Extension of Knowledge

After Adam and Eve eat the "fruit" from the Tree of Knowledge of Good and Evil, their eyes are "opened" to new awareness—including that awareness of each other. This knowledge could include an understanding of physical and emotional attraction, which might have been latent but unrecognised before.

The serpent's role in this awakening could involve subtle suggestions or observations, drawing Adam's attention to aspects of Eve's being— her physical form, her unique qualities, or the emotional connection they share. This newfound awareness could lead Adam to experience romantic attraction as a deeper connection than he had known before.

3.   The Serpent's Role in Shaping Human Desire

The serpent could be portrayed as emphasising the beauty of connection and intimacy. Through words or symbolic actions, it might show Adam how Eve's presence complements his own, planting seeds of desire and appreciation for their differences and unity.

This teaching could be framed not as a corruptive act but as one that introduces Adam to the complexity of human relationships. Romantic attraction, in this context, becomes part of the broader knowledge of good and evil—a mix of joy and struggle that reflects the human condition.

4.   The Dual Nature of Desire

The serpent's teachings might also carry a duality, reflecting the positive and negative aspects of romantic attraction. While it allows Adam to see Eve in a new light, appreciating her beauty and individuality, it also introduces vulnerabilities, such as longing, dependency, or insecurity.

This complexity mirrors the consequences of eating the forbidden fruit: what was once simple and harmonious now carries depth and weight, making their bond richer but also more fraught.

5.   Romantic Attraction as a Reflection of Divine Creation

The serpent's influence in teaching Adam about romantic attraction could also be seen as part of humanity's growth into being capable of love and relationship. By awakening Adam's awareness of Eve in this way, the serpent might unwittingly affirm the divine intention for humans to seek connection and unity, even in their fallen state.

In this interpretation, romantic attraction becomes a way for Adam and Eve to reflect the image of God through their relationship—a union that mirrors divine creativity and love.

6.   Symbolism of the Serpent as an Awakened Consciousness

The serpent's "teaching" could also be symbolic, representing the awakening of Adam's own consciousness. It does not need to directly instruct Adam but instead acts as a catalyst for him to see what was already there—his natural attraction and connection to Eve.

This awakening aligns with the broader theme of the Fall, where humanity transitions from innocence to awareness, gaining both the beauty and the burdens of knowledge.

7.   Romantic Attraction in the Context of Love and Sacrifice

As Adam begins to understand romantic attraction, it deepens his relationship with Eve. Their bond, once simple and unexamined, now becomes a source of joy, vulnerability, and strength, reflecting the profound complexity of human love.

This deeper connection sets the stage for their shared journey outside Eden, where their love must endure the trials of survival, parenthood, and loss. Romantic attraction, taught or awakened by the serpent, becomes a cornerstone of their partnership, giving them the emotional foundation to face a harsher world together.

THE SERPENT AS A CATALYST FOR LOVE'S COMPLEXITY

In this interpretation, the serpent acts as a symbol, awakening Adam to the depths of romantic attraction. The serpent introduces Adam to desire and complicity—changing his relationship with Eve into something richer, deeper. This narrative highlights that love encompasses both beauty and challenges, serving as a crucial part of human experiences from innocence to wisdom.

1.   Cain and Abel: The First Children

Cain was the firstborn, and he became a farmer, cultivating the land. Abel, his younger brother, took on the role of a shepherd. In Genesis 4, we find the story of Cain and Abel, an account of the earliest tragic conflict in human history. Both brothers brought offerings to God, but God favoured Abel's offering over Cain's. Enraged by jealousy, Cain killed Abel—marking the first murder in history. Later, God marked Cain as a wanderer so no one could kill him in revenge; he settled in the Land of Nod, east of Eden, where he started his own family.

Legacy: Cain is frequently seen as a symbolic figure representing jealousy, rivalry, and the complexity of moral choice. His descendants are mentioned briefly in Genesis, and he is noted as the ancestor of people who developed various trades and skills, such as metallurgy and music.

2.   Seth: The Third Son and the Lineage of Righteousness

After Abel's death, Adam and Eve had another son named Seth in continuity of righteousness. According to a verse from Genesis 4:25, Eve regarded Seth as a replacement for Abel. Seth became the ancestor of Noah, and through Noah, he is an ancestor to all humanity, as the Bible states that Noah's descendants repopulated the earth after the flood.

Legacy: Seth represents a lineage devoted to worshipping and following God. The Bible and other ancient traditions point out that the "line of Seth" is distinct for its righteousness and faithfulness, unlike Cain's lineage.

3.   Unnamed Sons and Daughters

Genesis 5:4 mentions that Adam and Eve had "other sons and daughters" beyond Cain, Abel, and Seth, though these children are not named or elaborated upon in the biblical text. Many ancient Jewish and Christian traditions speculate that Adam and Eve's children married each other to begin populating the world, as no other humans are mentioned at this time in the Genesis account.

Legacy: These unnamed sons and daughters represent the continuation of humanity, filling the earth and establishing the early generations of people. Various religious interpretations regard them as ancestors who helped populate the world and who formed distinct tribes and nations.

WHAT BECAME OF THEM?

The stories of Cain, Abel, and Seth reflect the trials and potential of early humanity. Cain's legacy is one marked by moral ambiguity—his descendants are known for technological and cultural advancements but are also separated from the righteous path symbolised by Seth's line. Seth's descendants, on the other hand, are often associated with piety and the worship of God, eventually leading to Noah, who preserved humanity through the flood.

In Jewish, Christian, and Islamic traditions, these descendants of Adam and Eve are seen as the forebears of all human societies. From the line of Seth came notable figures such as Noah, and, through generations, figures like Abraham, considered the father of faith in all three monotheistic religions.

EXTRA-BIBLICAL TRADITIONS AND INTERPRETATIONS

In some extra-biblical texts, like the Book of Jubilees and certain Gnostic texts, the story of Adam and Eve's family is expanded. For example:

The Book of Jubilees, a Jewish text, mentions two daughters of Adam and Eve named Awan and Azura. According to this text, Awan became the wife of Cain, and Azura married Seth.

Gnostic and early Christian traditions sometimes offer additional symbolic interpretations, portraying the children of Adam and Eve as representing various aspects of humanity's moral journey.

THE LEGACY OF ADAM AND EVE'S FAMILY

The descendants of Adam and Eve symbolise the diversity and complexity of human life. Through Cain's line, we see the emergence of human conflict, innovation, and divergence. Through Seth's line, we see a lineage devoted to faith and moral development, leading to the lineage of Noah and, by extension, the line that would bring about many central figures in the Abrahamic faiths.

In this manner, the family of Adam and Eve sets a foundation for the entire human story: capturing both moral struggles and innovations to faithfulness and redemption. The story of their family encapsulates humanity's potential for both good and evil, representing the range of choices, relationships, and legacies that define human existence.

WHAT *IF* THEY HADN'T MADE THE FATAL CHOICE?

Exploring an alternate timeline in which Adam and Eve choose not to eat the forbidden fruit offers a fascinating glimpse into a world untouched by sin and death. This scenario raises profound questions about free will, the nature of perfection, and the purpose of humanity.

THE POTENTIAL SIGNIFICANCE OF THE TREE OF LIFE

If Adam and Eve had never eaten from the Tree of Knowledge, the Tree of Life might have played a more significant role in their continued development. The Tree of Life could represent a path to gradual enlightenment, one in which Adam and Eve gain wisdom and understanding without the need for disobedience. Through communion with the Tree of Life, they might access divine knowledge at a pace aligned with their spiritual and moral growth. This process could preserve their innocence while allowing them to expand their understanding of creation and their purpose within it.

The Tree of Life might also symbolise the harmonious relationship between humanity and God, serving as a reminder that ultimate wisdom and eternal life are gifts bestowed through trust and alignment with divine will. This gradual enlightenment could contrast sharply with the abrupt and tumultuous knowledge gained from the Tree of Knowledge, offering a glimpse of what could have been a more balanced and peaceful evolution for humanity.

LIFE IN ETERNAL INNOCENCE

Without the Fall, Adam and Eve remain in a state of innocence, living forever in the garden. They enjoy perfect communion with God, harmony with nature, and a pure relationship unmarred by shame or conflict. However, this idyllic existence comes at a cost: the absence of knowledge and growth. They remain childlike, unable to fully understand the complexities of good and evil.

THE NATURE OF FREE WILL

Their choice not to eat the fruit raises questions about free will. Are they totally free if they never disobey? Perhaps God occasionally assesses their obedience to ensure their choice is genuine. Alternatively, their continued obedience might reflect a deeper understanding of trust and submission, rather than a lack of autonomy.

THE ABSENCE OF DEATH

Without sin, there is no death. Adam and Eve's descendants live forever, creating a paradise that grows more populated over time. However, the lack of death introduces practical and philosophical challenges. How does the garden accommodate an ever-increasing population? Does the absence of mortality diminish the value of life?

THE DEVELOPMENT OF KNOWLEDGE

If Adam and Eve remain in Eden, how do they acquire knowledge? Perhaps God imparts wisdom gradually, allowing them to grow without the corruption of sin. This gradual enlightenment could lead to a more profound understanding of creation, fostering innovation and progress within the bounds of perfection.

THE ROLE OF THE SERPENT

In this scenario—*if they didn't eat the fruit*—the serpent's role takes on a different significance. Its failure to tempt Adam and Eve might lead it to question its purpose. Does it continue to seek opportunities for mischief, or does it retreat into obscurity? Alternatively, the serpent might find redemption, becoming a guardian or guide within the garden.

THE PURPOSE OF HUMANITY

Without the Fall, the purpose of humanity remains unclear. Do Adam and Eve's descendants exist solely to worship God and tend the garden, or do they have a greater role in creation? This question touches on the broader themes of destiny, purpose, and the nature of a perfect existence.

REFLECTIONS ON THE ALTERNATE TIMELINE

Imagining a world without the Fall offers a thought-provoking contrast to the actual narrative. It highlights the value of knowledge, the complexity of free will, and the profound consequences of choice. While this alternate timeline may seem idyllic, it also underscores the richness of the human experience, with its blend of joy, sorrow, growth, and redemption.

In the garden, Adam and Eve had an intimate, constant, and immediate relationship with God. Beyond the garden, their connection with God took on a different form: less immediate, more distant.

God now appears less interested in humanity's problems, and is less approachable, representing the human search for purpose and contact in a world with less immediate divine instruction. This shift signifies the human spirituality's quest to make sense of, and find divinity in, life's struggles.

This became a metaphor for the human condition: struggling to find meaning, faith, and connectedness in a world where God is less immediately involved, and prayers seem either ignored or remain unanswered. This shift signifies humanity's search of spirituality and meaning amidst the difficulties of life.

SUMMARY / CONCLUSION:

In "Adam and Eve in the Garden", the timeless story of Adam and Eve is reimagined as a deeply human and passionate love story. Set in Eden, their relationship starts innocently and develops into a connection based on mutual tenderness, desire, and exploration. They are not just the first man and woman—they are the first lovers.

But paradise is not without its trials. When Eve's curiosity draws her toward the forbidden fruit, and Adam chooses love over obedience, their world is forever changed. Their expulsion from Eden could have shattered them, but instead, it becomes the crucible in which their love is strengthened.

Together, they face the wilderness beyond Eden's gates, building a life with only each other to lean on. Their love, tested and refined, leads to the birth of their son, Cain—the firstborn of humanity. Their union brings life to the world.

Adam and Eve's story is more than a tale of loss; it is a story of the Creation; of how love endures through hardship and becomes the foundation upon which humanity is built. From their love, all people come forth. Their choice to hold on to each other in the face of the unknown is what gave birth to the generations that followed.

Their relationship represents the genesis from which all of humanity was born.

SUCH IS GOD'S LOVE – A POEM

The rain comes down
In fine droplets.
And soon the frown
Dissolves to let
The farmer's face
Shine on with grace…
The hot-bellied
Earth, once buried
In Wait and Hope,
Now wakes to sip
Its fill of this
Sudden blessing…
Such is God's Love!
It rains and pours
On rich and poor…
God also cares
For those whose tears
Speak of their pain
And their sorrow…
We can swallow
God's soothing Rain
To stop the pain…

This Book ends in Praise to God and in the
words of the Psalmist (Psalm 147):

Praise God, from whom all blessings flow.
Praise Him, all creatures here below.
Praise Him above, ye heav'nly host.
Praise Father, Son, and Holy Ghost!

***

"May the Lord bless you and protect you. May the Lord smile on you and
be gracious to you." Numbers 6:24 to 26.

RESOURCES

Please check out these products/services by clicking on each link. We are compensated by Amazon for promoting their products. This is how we can give discounts to our customers/partners when they purchase our books.

Amazon Best Sellers in Children's Books https://amzn.to/41x2DxX

Best Sellers in Kindle Store https://amzn.to/4kysazs

Best Sellers in Health, Fitness & Dieting https://amzn.to/3FcfiyY

Best Sellers in Foreign & International Law https://amzn.to/4bvMDkm

Best Sellers in Legal Self-Help https://amzn.to/3DqBZir

Best Sellers in Libros en Espanol https://amzn.to/3DlcoYe

Best Sellers in Literature & Fiction https://amzn.to/4i4mo7c

Best Sellers in Medical Books https://amzn.to/3D9LBhy

Best Sellers in Mystery, Thriller & Suspense https://amzn.to/43qYZIy

Best Sellers in Textbooks: New, Used & Rental Textbooks https://amzn.to/41yISGe

Best Sellers in Teen & Young Adult Books https://amzn.to/3FaD9PE

Best Sellers in Test Preparation https://amzn.to/4hgeMgA

Best Sellers in Travel https://amzn.to/41uu0Zx

Best Sellers in Patio, Lawn & Garden https://amzn.to/41Lp6IZ

Best Sellers in Pet Supplies https://amzn.to/4ivrLMm

Best Sellers in Software https://amzn.to/3F9j7F8

Best Sellers in Sports Collectibles https://amzn.to/4bzpuh3

Best Sellers in Tools & Home Improvement https://amzn.to/43s9bjZ

Best Sellers in Toys & Games https://amzn.to/4bzpNIJ

Best Sellers in Christian Books & Bibles https://amzn.to/43ru0Mw

Best Sellers in Relationships, Parenting & Personal Development https://amzn.to/3Xw0n8Y

***

CITATIONS

Al-Badarneh, A. "Milton's Pro-Feminist Presentation of Eve in Paradise Lost," International Journal of Applied Linguistics & English Literature, 3(4) (2014): 105-109. https://doi.org/10.7575/aiac.ijalel.v.3n.4p.105.

Arbel, V. "Guarding His Body, Mourning His Death, and Pleading for Him in Heaven: On Adam's Death and Eve's Virtues in the Greek Life of Adam and Eve," 103-126 in Coming Back to Life: The Permeability of Past and Present, Mortality and Immortality, Death and Life in the Ancient Mediterranean, edited by Frederick S. Tappenden and Carly Daniel Hughes, with the assistance of Bradley N. Rice. Montreal, QC: McGill University Library, 2017. https://doi.org/10.2307/j.ctvmx3k11.11.

Davis, M. "Exiled Poetics," Art/Research International: A Transdisciplinary Journal, 7(2) (2022): 351-368. https://doi.org/10.18432/ari29676.

Houwelingen, P.H.R. "Power Play in the Church? The Case of 1 Timothy 2:8–15," Verbum Christi Jurnal Teologi Reformed Injili, 6(2), (2019): 159-185. https://doi.org/10;/.51688/vc6.2.2019.art5.

Osman, M. "The Adam and Eve Story as Exemplar of an Early-Life Variant of the Oedipus Complex," Journal of the American Psychoanalytic Association, 48(4), (2000): 1295-1325. https://doi.org/10.1177/00030651 000480041901.

Osman, M. "The Role of an Early-Life Variant of the Oedipus Complex in Motivating Religious Endeavors," Journal of the American Psychoanalytic Association, 52(4), (2004): 975-997. https://doi.org/10.1177/000306510 40520041601.

Özsert, S. "Yaratiliş Hikayesinin Farkli Bir Okumasi: Feminist Perspektiften Geleneksel Anlatilarda Adem, Havva Ve Yilan," The Journal of Academic Social Science Studies, Year: 16 - Number: 96, (2023): 79-90. https://doi. org.

Paice, Rosamund. "'Domestick Adam' versus 'Adventurous Eve': Arguments about Gardening in Milton's Eden," Milton Studies, 63(2), (2021): 265. https://doi.org/10.5325/miltonstudies.63.2.0265.

Servin, S. "Paradise Lost: Difference between Adam and Eve's Lament on Leaving Paradise—A Contrastive Analysis," K Ta, 15(2), (2013): https://doi.org/10.9744/kata.15.2.85-92.

Wagner-Tsukamoto, S. "The Tree of Life: Banned or Not Banned? A Rational Choice Interpretation," Scandinavian Journal of the Old Testament, 26(1), (2012): 102-122. https://doi.org/10.1080/09018328.2012.704211.

Woodford, B. "The Freedom Dilemma: Milton's (and Adam's) Inability to Reconcile Reason and Authority," Literature & History, 31(2), (2022): 119-133. https://doi.org/10.1177/03061973221139270.

Yi, X. "Science and Art in the Creation of Adam," Journal of Education Humanities and Social Sciences, 11, (2023): 149-154. https://doi.org/10.54097/ehss.v11i.7541

Here are some references that can provide further reading and context on the topics discussed, such as human origins, early civilisation, the Genesis narrative, and population growth. These resources include scientific, historical, and theological perspectives and provide a well-rounded view of human population development from multiple disciplines, bridging religious, scientific, and historical insights into a fuller understanding of humanity's growth and diversity.

SCIENTIFIC AND HISTORICAL PERSPECTIVES ON HUMAN ORIGINS AND POPULATION GROWTH

Diamond, J. *Guns, Germs, and Steel: The Fates of Human Societies.* W. W. Norton & Company, 1997.

Examines the factors that allowed certain civilisations to expand and dominate, impacting population growth and human migration patterns.

Harari, Y. N. *Sapiens: A Brief History of Humankind*. Harper, 2015.

Explores the development of human societies, the Agricultural Revolution, and the evolution of human culture from ancient to modern times.

Mithen, S. *After the Ice: A Global Human History, 20,000-5000 BC*. Harvard University Press, 2003.

Focuses on human societies during and after the last Ice Age, detailing how early humans adapted and expanded their populations across the world.

Reich, D. *Who We Are and How We Got Here: Ancient DNA and the New Science of the Human Past*. Pantheon Books, 2018.

Covers genetic discoveries about human history, including interbreeding of Homo sapiens with Neanderthals and Denisovans, and how these findings contribute to understanding population diversity.

Renfrew, C. and P. Bahn. *Archaeology: Theories, Methods, and Practice*. Thames & Hudson, 2008.

An introductory text on archaeology that covers the evolution of human societies and how archaeological evidence informs our understanding of population growth and migrations.

Stringer, C. and R. McKie. *African Exodus: The Origins of Modern Humanity*. Henry Holt & Company, 1996.

A look at the origins of Homo sapiens and the "Out of Africa" theory, detailing the migration and genetic history of human populations.

THEOLOGICAL PERSPECTIVES ON GENESIS AND HUMAN POPULATION

Alter, R. *The Five Books of Moses: A Translation with Commentary*. W. W. Norton & Company, 2004.

Offers a scholarly translation of the first five books of the Bible, beginning with Genesis, with commentary that delves into the literary and cultural context of these ancient texts.

Collins, C. J. *Did Adam and Eve Really Exist? Who They Were and Why You Should Care.* Crossway, 2011.

A discussion of the historical and theological significance of Adam and Eve, examining various interpretations of the Genesis account.

Enns, P. *The Evolution of Adam: What the Bible Does and Doesn't Say about Human Origins.* Brazos Press, 2012.

Examines the Genesis narrative from a theological perspective and addresses how it might be reconciled with modern scientific understandings of human origins.

Sarna, N. M. *Genesis: The JPS Torah Commentary.* Jewish Publication Society, 1989.

A comprehensive commentary on the book of Genesis from a Jewish perspective, exploring themes of human relationships, divine purpose, and population.

Stump, J. B. and S. N. Gundry, eds. *Four Views on Creation, Evolution, and Intelligent Design.* Zondervan, 2017.

A comparative look at various Christian perspectives on creation, including discussions on the historical Adam and Eve and interpretations of Genesis.

Walton, J. H. *The Lost World of Genesis One: Ancient Cosmology and the Origins Debate.* IVP Academic, 2009.

A theological exploration of Genesis that interprets the creation narrative within its ancient Near Eastern context, providing insights into how early humans might have understood their origins.

POPULATION GENETICS AND ANTHROPOLOGY

Cann, R. L., M. Stoneking, and A. C. Wilson. "Mitochondrial DNA and Human Evolution," *Nature*, 325(6099), 1987: 31-36.

A foundational paper in population genetics that supports the theory of human migration out of Africa and contributes to understanding human population development.

Henn, B. M., L. L. Cavalli-Sforza, and M. W. Feldman. "The Great Human Expansion," *Proceedings of the National Academy of Sciences*, 109(Supplement 1), 2012: 17758-17764.

Discusses the genetic evidence for human migration and expansion, contributing to the understanding of how the world's population developed over millennia.

Schurr, T. G. and S. T. Sherry. "Mitochondrial DNA and Y Chromosome Diversity and the Peopling of the Americas: Evolutionary and Demographic Evidence," *American Journal of Human Biology*, 16(4), 2004: 420-439.

Focuses on how genetic diversity explains population distribution and development, particularly in the Americas.

ABOUT THE AUTHOR

Chukky Daniels is a researcher, storyteller, poet, educator, business consultant, philanthropist, and digital creator who dares to challenge conventional narratives. In *Adam & Eve in the Garden: A Twenty-First Century Love Story*, readers are invited to explore timeless themes of love, choice, family, temptation, and humanity through a fresh perspective.

If you have comments or questions; or would like to suggest ways to improve the content of the book for the next edition; or would like to give the author ideas to be considered for inclusion in the planned sequel, please forward your information to the author using this email address: chukky@ adamandevebooks.com. You would be contacted as soon as the sequel is published; and hopefully, some of you will be thrilled to see your suggestions in the book!